The Retreat

TRUSTING HIM

L.M. SOMERTON

Trusting Him
ISBN # 978-1-78686-391-1
©Copyright L.M. Somerton 2019
Cover Art by Melody Pond ©Copyright April 2019
Interior text design by Claire Siemaszkiewicz
Pride Publishing

Pride Publishing books by L.M. Somerton

Single title
Mountain Rescue
Black Dog
The Portrait
Stroke Rate
Chemical Bonds
Testing Lysander
Owned by the Sea

The Wyverns
Mantrap
Deathtrap
Rattrap
Sand Trap
Steel Trap

Tales from the Edge
Reaching the Edge
Living on the Edge
Dancing on the Edge
A Double-Edged Sword
Rough Around the Edges
Scorched Edges
Driven to the Edge
Binding the Edges

Investigating Love
Rasputin's Kiss
Evil's Embrace
Tarot's Love

Warlocks
Elemental Love
Elemental Hope

The Retreat
Serving Him
Trusting Him

Fairground Attractions
Ghost Train
Merry-go-Round

Anthologies
Racing Hearts: Keeping the Luck
His Rules: Tagging Mackenzie

TRUSTING HIM

Dedication

For all my friends in the BDSM community,
thank you.

Chapter One

The mellow notes of Smokestack Lightning gave the atmosphere in the club a relaxed vibe, the volume not too high to make the music intrusive. Luke ran a finger through the condensation coating his tumbler of iced water. A slice of lime jostled for space with ice cubes riding on bubbles of carbonation, its color a splash of neon brightness in the dim light. He breathed deeply, taking in the scent of leather and wax furniture polish. The Underground's Friday lunchtime crowd filled the tables around him and he caught the edges of innocuous conversations about jobs and families and holidays. A love of kink didn't wipe away the mundane, everyday aspects of life, though it did make them a little more interesting.

Luke watched a young submissive, kneeling next to his Master's chair, rest his head on the Dominant's thigh. The sub's expression when the Dom ruffled his hair was one of pure bliss. Luke wondered, as he often did, what it would feel like to put that expression on another man's face. He couldn't imagine anything more satisfying. Caring for somebody who wanted to be cared for, who craved his attention and guidance, was something that Luke could only aspire to. He hoped that one day the right man would come along and he'd get the chance to live the lifestyle he desired, but it hadn't happened yet.

He sipped his drink, wondering at his own contemplative mood. It wasn't like him to mope over what he didn't yet have. He fancied that his job as general manager of The Retreat put him in a position where he could witness too many loving D/s relationships and it was beginning to have an effect on his psyche.

He knew the moment Carey Hoffman came into the dining room. There was a subtle change in the atmosphere and a slight rise in the noise level as staff and club members offered their greetings and exchanged the latest news. Carey was the definition of enigmatic. He had a powerful presence that drew people's attention—they wanted him to notice them. Immaculate as always in a dark suit, light blue shirt and patterned tie, Carey strolled across the room with purpose, pausing now and again for a few words with people he knew well. Those he was less familiar with got a nod of acknowledgment at the very least. Nobody was excluded. His attitude was fundamental to the club's success. Even the newest member was made to feel at home.

Carey arrived at Luke's table and Luke stood to greet him, offering his hand. To his surprise, he found himself pulled into an embrace.

"It's great to see you, Luke. I've been remiss in keeping up with your news. Life's so busy, it's difficult to get down to Hampshire as often as I'd like." Carey took a seat at the table.

"It's hectic for both of us. I hope my weekly reports have given you all the information you need about happenings at The Retreat."

"They have, and I couldn't be more pleased with the way you're running things. I've had nothing but praise from customers who have dropped into the club after their stay, as well as emails and phone calls, all singing your praises. Tor's cooking gets no end of compliments. The only thing close to a complaint I've had is men saying they put on weight during their stay."

"I can understand that," Luke said. "I have to ration myself or I'd be spending five hours a day in the gym on top of running every morning."

Carey chuckled. "It's fortunate for me that I have Alistair to make sure I keep in trim. There's nothing like a young, willing submissive to keep a man active."

"I'm sure. Is he around today? I'd like to say hello."

"I'm afraid not. He has a new show opening next week at a small gallery in Mayfair. He's over there setting everything up. No doubt he'll get back later, flustered and stressed out—you'll see him then. He's excited that you're staying over with us."

"And you'll be right here to calm him down."

"One of my favorite jobs." Carey gestured toward the nearest server, who came scurrying over.

"What can I get you, Sir?" The young man bounced on his bare toes, arse jiggling beneath his short leather kilt.

"My usual please, Gordy. Luke, would you like a refill?"

"Please." Luke swallowed the last of his drink and handed the glass to Gordy, who skipped toward the bar. "Is he always that energetic?"

"I'm afraid so," Carey said, his tone wry. "He needs a good Dom to wear him out a bit. He makes me tired watching him."

The fresh drinks were soon delivered and Luke settled back in his chair. "So, I assume you're going to tell me why you called me up here? Not that I object to the change of scenery."

"Yes, I suppose I should. I wanted to talk to you about the big group you have arriving next week and your requirements for additional staff."

"There are five couples coming, all members of the Manchester club Collars and Cuffs. They're staying for five days and have a few theme nights planned, which should be exciting. They're bringing their own costumes but have ordered some interesting outfits for the houseboys. Tor is matching his menus to their themes. He has a full complement of catering staff — two assistants. I think you know Benjy and Frank because they've done a stint here too. He has requested a dedicated server to help out. Normally Tor or his kitchen assistants wait on the guests, but with this number of people he thinks they'll be too busy. I reckon one person should be enough. I still have two houseboys in residence — Fergus and Henry, who were both approved by the guests — and Rayne will be in his usual role as chauffeur. I have two additional cars on call should they be needed and Rayne has access to a minibus if they all want to go on an outing together. But you know all this from the plan I sent you." Luke gave him a quizzical glance. "I was hoping you had some news for me about a potential server."

"I'm going to send Goran down to run the bar, keep things stocked and generally help out," Carey said.

"He'll be a very welcome addition. I can leave him to get on with that side of things—he certainly doesn't need my interference. But he's not a server."

"He can deal with the wine, but I have someone else in mind for table and room service. I have a young man here who has been helping out, but he's a little nervous. The noise and the number of people in the club can be a bit overwhelming at times."

"Does he have any other experience?" Luke asked, his curiosity piqued.

"Silver service training at a restaurant with two Michelin stars. He's been taught to be invisible and he's good at it."

"A sub?"

"Yes. He has huge potential. He hasn't played with anyone yet but I've seen him watching. He's interested. I don't suppose he would have applied for a job here if he wasn't, but he's still finding his feet and he's shy. I think it would give his confidence a boost if he went down to The Retreat for a while. With your guidance, he'll have time to work out what it is he wants in a less intimidating environment."

"He sounds ideal. Do I get to meet him?"

"Of course. That's why you're here."

"Just one thing," Luke said. "If he's nervous, is he going to be okay with the dress code?"

"He understands it's a condition of the role. He hasn't had a problem with the uniform here as you'll see." Carey waved at Gordy, who immediately came to his side.

"Has Skye arrived for his shift yet?"

"Yes, Sir. He's getting changed, I think. He'll be out in a minute or two."

"When he's ready, ask him to come over and join us please."

Gordy took off at a run and Carey rolled his eyes. "I'm amazed that boy doesn't fall headlong over the furniture, or someone's legs. He moves like a jack rabbit."

"Someone needs to put him on a leash."

"Indeed. I don't think it will be that long before they do. He has a sweet nature and I've had a few enquiries about him. Ah." Carey glanced over his shoulder. "Here's Skye now."

It wasn't dignified, but Luke twisted around in his seat to take a look at his potential employee as he wound his way between the tables. He hadn't formed an impression of what Skye might look like, but the reality was better than anything Luke's imagination could have conjured. Skye was slight, delicate, maybe five feet six or seven, no more. His skin was lightly tan, a coloring that Luke guessed came from his heritage rather than the sun. He had no tattoos that Luke could see and considering that all he wore was a short leather kilt, that didn't leave much room to hide any. The wavy hair Luke had assumed was pale blond was in fact silver-gray, though the boy's eyelashes and brows were a much darker shade, which made Luke wonder if the silver was natural.

Skye stopped in front of the table facing Luke and Carey. He clasped his hands behind his back and ducked his head. "Gordy said you wanted to see me, Mr. Hoffman." Skye's voice was so soft Luke had to concentrate to catch his words.

"I did, Skye. You remember I spoke to you about a job at The Retreat in Hampshire?"

Nodding, Skye darted a quick look at Luke. Luke caught a glimpse of violet-blue eyes before Skye focused his gaze on the carpet once more.

"Well, this is Mr. Redding. He's in charge of The Retreat. I want you to wait on us over lunchtime and show him what you can do."

"Hello, Skye," Luke said, keeping his voice low and trying to project reassurance. "I hear you've had excellent training. We have a mixture of guests staying at The Retreat, but they all have something in common. They love their food. We have a dedicated chef and customers can pick their own menus and eat as much as they want. That means a lot of serving both at table and in the guests' rooms. Do you think you can handle that?"

Skye scuffed his bare toes into the carpet. "Yes, Sir."

"And you understand that The Retreat caters for men who are in the BDSM lifestyle, just like here at the club?" Skye nodded and a light pink flush bloomed on his cheekbones. "Sometimes, you might be required to wear very little or nothing at all. Does that worry you?"

"No, Sir." Skye's response was barely audible.

Luke wanted to make eye contact with the shy young man but Skye kept his gaze lowered.

"Remove your kilt, Skye," Carey ordered.

Luke tightened his grip on his drink. He expected Skye to bolt but instead he undid the buckle at his hip, let the leather garment drop to the floor then stepped out of it.

"Hands behind your back," Carey instructed.

Luke glanced around the restaurant. Almost every man in the place had turned to watch. Skye stood absolutely still, clad only in the mesh thong that was issued to all the serving staff at The Underground to wear under their kilts.

"Fetch two menus, please."

Luke watched, entranced, as Skye walked away, hips swaying. He might as well have been naked for all the coverage his underwear gave him. He had natural grace and if it weren't for the slight tension in his shoulders, Luke might have believed he was entirely comfortable following Carey's orders.

"You're testing him. Why?" Luke didn't take his eyes away from Skye as he collected two menus and returned to the table.

"Because you need to be confident that he will do as you ask, when he'd prefer to run and hide."

"He's attracting a lot of attention."

"Are you surprised?"

"Not at all. He's stunning."

Carey's smile turned into a smirk. "Then you can handle him from now on."

Luke accepted the menu Skye handed him. He pointed to a spot on the carpet next to his chair. "You'll only be serving us, Skye. Kneel here while we make our choices."

Skye hurried to do as he was asked. He dropped to his knees next to Luke's chair, resting his hands palms down on his thighs, his arse on his heels. Luke found it extremely difficult to concentrate on the menu selection. The printed letters kept dancing a jig in front of his eyes.

"The chef here makes fantastic risotto," Carey offered.

"Then I'll have that. Anything you recommend is bound to be good," Luke said, relieved not to have to think about it any further.

"I'll have the same," Carey said. "Bring a selection of chef's appetizers while we wait for the main course."

Skye raised his eyes, looking to Luke for permission to move. Luke got his first complete view of Skye's eyes, which were a startling, unusual color. They, combined with his silver hair and delicate features, made him beautiful.

"You may go." Luke handed both menus back to Skye. He noticed that the young man's hands were trembling as he took the leather-bound *cartes du jour*, but he was steady on his feet as he walked back to the kitchen. "He's got courage."

"The orders make him brave. They give him enough focus to get past his embarrassment."

Luke nodded. "I'll have him stay with us while we eat. Kneeling will give him some protection."

Carey grinned but didn't say anything.

"What?"

"He's imprinting on you. You're his safe place now."

Luke shook his head. "You planned this all along, didn't you?"

"I'm admitting to nothing."

Smug suited Carey, much to Luke's annoyance. He found himself scanning the restaurant, eager for Skye's return. It was a few minutes before he emerged from the kitchen, a large plate of appetizers in his hands. When he bent to place them on the low table in front of Luke's seat, there were several sharp intakes of breath from diners at the surrounding tables. Luke glared at their occupants.

"You may put your kilt back on, Skye."

Not bothering to hide his relief, Skye buckled the garment around his hips. "Thank you, Sir." He resumed his position kneeling next to Luke's chair.

Grinning, Carey took a breaded prawn from the appetizer platter. "Eat something, Luke. I can't manage all this food on my own. We'll move to a proper dining table when the main course is ready."

"Do you have any allergies, Skye?" Luke asked. Confusion shadowed Skye's pretty face. "It's an easy enough question," Luke reprimanded. "I expect an answer."

"No, Sir. I'm not allergic to anything."

"Any strong dislikes? I'm talking about food here."

"Nothing too spicy, Sir."

Luke hid a smile. He selected a miniature blini, topped with a slither of smoked salmon and some cream cheese, from the plate then held it to Skye's plump lips. Skye opened for him, accepting the treat. Luke fed him a few more appetizers before taking anything for himself. Skye's quiet moans of satisfaction were enough to make Luke hard, something he didn't try to hide. Every now and again he caught Carey giving him a knowing glance. Luke's boss was enjoying every moment of the scene he had engineered.

"Find us a table for the main course, please, Skye." Luke ordered. "I'd like a glass of white wine to go with the risotto, something light. You may ask the barman for advice on a suitable choice. Carey, would you like another drink with lunch?"

"I'll have the same."

"Two glasses then, please. Then you may check on progress in the kitchen. Take the wine straight to the table."

Once Skye had risen and moved away to complete his tasks, Luke turned to Carey. "What exactly do you have planned, Carey?"

"Skye needs a Master, and you need someone to train. A Dom without a sub is an empty shell."

"Very philosophical. And do you not think I'm capable of finding the right man myself?"

"Frankly, my friend, no." Carey chuckled. "Ninety-nine percent of the time, you're stuck down in Hampshire, in the middle of nowhere, surrounded by men with their own partners. I don't think Rayne or the houseboys are your type, and Tor keeps his kitchen assistants firmly chained to the stove. You have little opportunity to hunt down a good sub. You're an excellent manager and I don't want to lose you. Skye will keep you well occupied."

"I never pegged you as a matchmaker, Carey. I'm appalled."

"No, you're not. You're intrigued. You're already feeling protective. Where's the harm? Take him back to Hampshire with you tomorrow, put him to work and see where things go. Train him. He probably won't even realize you're doing it."

"He's very young."

"He is. This is his first job after graduating. He got his other experience working part-time while he was a student. It's all the more reason that he should find his way under the guidance of someone experienced. The Underground is a safe space, but sooner or later his curiosity is going to get him into the sort of trouble he won't be able to handle."

The thought of Skye venturing into the world of Dominance and submission without protection sent a cold shiver down Luke's spine. "Perhaps it is time," he murmured. "Fine. I'll take him back to The Retreat. But don't think you've heard the last of this, Carey. Wait till I tell Alistair about your meddling."

"Who do you think is really behind this?" Carey chuckled. "Alistair will be delighted that his plan has worked. Be warned, the sub mafia is a powerful organization with a long reach."

Luke sighed. "Someone needs to put that in the BDSM manual in big red letters. There are a lot of unsuspecting, innocent Doms out there ready to get hooked."

"Indeed. How about we contemplate our vulnerability over some good food and wine?"

Deciding alcohol might be a good idea as he didn't have to drive anywhere, Luke followed Carey to the table Skye had selected for them. He needed a distraction from silver hair and big violet eyes before he did something he might regret.

Chapter Two

Skye cast surreptitious glances at the handsome, stern man behind the wheel. Luke Redding's Lexus was the nicest car Skye had ever ridden in. The tantalizing smell of leather tickled his nostrils as he tried to make himself as small and inconspicuous as possible. The thought of being responsible for such a luxurious vehicle gave Skye palpitations. He was much more at home driving his grandfather's beaten-up, thirty-year-old Land Rover around the farm. It smelled of sheep, dogs and manure.

"Something you're thinking about made you smile," Luke said. "Want to tell me about it?"

He didn't take his eyes off the road, but there was an air of expectancy about his silence. Skye nibbled his lower lip, wondering if he should lie and make up something glamorous. "I was thinking about the smell of wet sheep, Sir." He blurted the words before he could stop himself.

"I'm intrigued." Luke checked his mirrors before joining the steady flow of motorway traffic.

"I grew up on a farm, Sir. Private land so I was driving all kinds of stuff by the time I was fourteen, but I usually drove in wellies. In your car, I feel like I should take my shoes off." He lifted his feet, checking he hadn't left any traces of dirt on the pristine carpets.

"I have a cousin who keeps a herd of Aberdeen Angus beef cattle in the Highlands," Luke said. "It's a tough life, but very rewarding."

"My grandad keeps sheep in Somerset, some of them rare breeds, on the edge of Exmoor."

"And your parents? Where are they?"

"My mum died when I was very young, Sir. A hereditary condition that made her susceptible to infection. I grew up on my grandparents' farm." Skye didn't remember his mother at all. It had always been him and his dad, Batman and Robin, supported by his hardworking grandparents.

"And your father?"

"Gone, Sir." The inexorable creep of sadness enveloped Skye. Talking about his dad was still a raw, open wound.

"I'm sorry. I didn't mean to upset you." Luke frowned. "You don't have to tell me anything you don't want to."

Skye stared out of the window, not sure whether to explain. Luke tapped one finger on the leather-wrapped steering wheel.

"You know, you don't have to call me Sir, Skye. Unless you want to. Mr. Redding is fine."

"If you don't mind, I'll stick with Sir. It feels right." That was one of the few things Skye was sure about. It hadn't occurred to him to call Luke anything else. He was grateful that Luke had changed the subject—a deliberate kindness he suspected.

"Then that's fine. Tell me, Skye, what do you hope to get out of working at The Retreat?"

"I'm very grateful for the opportunity, Sir."

"That isn't what I asked you, though, is it?" Luke's demeanor didn't change. He didn't seem angry.

"Sorry." All Skye's bravery crumbled. He chewed on a fingernail.

"Stop that," Luke ordered. "No more biting nails or gnawing on your lip. I expect an answer to the question, Skye."

Tears welled in Skye's eyes at the thought that he had already managed to disappoint Luke. He fought them back. He couldn't imagine Luke had an ounce of patience for a blubbering, emotional sub.

"I want to find out what kind of submissive I am, Sir."

"And you haven't had the chance to explore that yet, have you?"

"No," Skye whispered. "I watched…at The Underground. Tried to understand, but it was all so confusing."

"Well, The Retreat is a good place to start. You'll see submission in all its forms amongst our guests, from full-time slaves to men who just like the occasional foray into bondage. There are as many kinds of submission as there are submissives."

"And Dominants, Sir?" A small grain of Skye's courage returned.

"Yes, Dominants too. The lifestyle isn't a one-size-fits-all kind of thing."

"Alistair said you'd help me, look after me. He said you were patient. I'll try my best, I promise."

"And I won't ask for anything more. While you're under my care, I'll do what I can to guide you. But you have to understand that decisions about what you want in the future will have to come from you, Skye. I'll give you the structure you need to make them in your own time, but I won't be able to make them for you."

"I'm a good server, Sir. I enjoy the routine of it, but it's not what I want to be forever. I have a degree in history. I'd like to be a researcher someday."

"I have an interest in military history," Luke said. "Something I studied at Dartmouth."

"You were in the navy, Sir?" Skye wasn't surprised. Luke had the posture and manner of an officer.

"For fifteen years. I resigned my commission to take care of my father. After Dad died, Mr. Hoffman offered me the management role at The Retreat. I already knew him through The Underground. It turned out to be a good move. I love the peace and quiet of the New Forest."

"I think I'll like it too. It will be more like home. London is noisy," Skye said. "It scares me. Everyone at The Underground was kind to me, but I felt out of place, like I didn't quite fit."

"How did you find the job at the club in the first place?"

"I had a friend at university who told me about it. He had a boyfriend who fancied himself as a Dom who was a member."

"Fancied himself?"

"He wasn't the real thing, Sir."

"You can tell?"

"True Dominants have this aura of certainty about them, Sir. Like they're in control of everything around them and aren't afraid of anything. They don't have to shout or show off. It's in their eyes, their mannerisms and expressions. It's not one thing—it's a special combination. Not many men have it. A lot just play at it." Skye gulped, shocked at his runaway tongue. "I shouldn't assume to know anything about it..."

"Why not? Who better to recognize a true Dominant than a true submissive? The same thing applies in reverse, you know — there's something unique about a true, natural submissive. It's a very special thing to place your trust in another man. Submission is a gift and you shouldn't give yours carelessly."

It was advice, not a reprimand. Skye thought handing control to Luke wouldn't be difficult at all — it would be a relief. Responsibility for big decisions made him anxious whereas Luke wouldn't blink twice. He wondered what kind of body Luke hid beneath his shirt and tie. He had broad shoulders and narrow hips. Slender fingers gripped the steering wheel. He had a young face — Skye guessed he was around his mid-thirties but couldn't be sure. He was certain that Luke's handsome, if stern features appealed to him. A lot. He'd dreamt about him the previous night for the few hours he had managed to sleep. Luke had stayed over with Mr. Hoffmann and Alistair then picked Skye up just after lunch. It had been easy enough for Skye to pack his few things as he'd been staying with two of the other subs from the club while he saved some money. They had cried and hugged him but wished him the very best of luck, promising him the tiny box room again if he ever needed it.

Luke flexed his fingers on the wheel and Skye's thoughts reverted to the present. He couldn't help but wonder what those fingers would feel like wrapped around his wrist, or, better still, his dick. He shifted in his seat, thankful that the hoodie he wore hid his misbehaving cock.

"While you are under my control, Skye, you won't be allowed to come without my permission."

Skye glimpsed a brief smile, but it was gone as soon as it appeared. "I'm twenty-two, Sir." Skye thought that should be enough to explain why Luke was asking the impossible.

"Which is why, when we get back to The Retreat, I'll be fitting you with a chastity device. I don't expect miracles."

"A ch...ch..."

"Chastity is the word you're looking for, Skye."

Skye took a few deep breaths. Hyperventilation was a distinct possibility. He recognized the irony that just the idea of a cock cage made him want to come even more. "Oh God..."

"It's nothing to be afraid of, Skye."

"No, Sir. It's not that. I just wish you'd waited a while to tell me." Skye pressed both hands over his groin. This time Luke did smile. A low chuckle followed.

"Like that idea, huh? You see—we're already uncovering your kinks. I think further discussion should wait until later, though, don't you?"

"Yes! I mean, yes please, Sir." The rest of the journey was going to be excruciating enough.

* * * *

Luke did his familiar tour of The Retreat on automatic pilot, more concerned about Skye's reaction than about describing every detail. His new charge was quiet, his eyes getting wider at every new revelation. He seemed most excited by the dungeon, but Luke made this assumption based only on the way Skye's glance flickered from one piece of equipment to another, because he didn't speak unless Luke asked him a direct question. By the time they returned to Luke's office, Skye was unable to keep still. He fidgeted, moving his weight from foot to foot.

Luke took the seat behind his desk. He steepled his fingers, debating how to begin. It was nothing more than a feeling, but he thought Skye would respond best to strict rules and discipline. He didn't want to coddle him, but he was also cognizant of Skye's inexperience and his innocence. He decided to go with his gut.

"Take your clothes off, Skye. Fold them and put them on the desk." He made sure his tone was firm. He wanted it to sound like an order, not a request.

Skye took a shuddering breath but did as he was asked. Shoes and socks first, then his jeans and shirt. He wore plain black boxer briefs, tented by an eager erection. Luke was happy to see such a positive reaction to a simple command and, though Skye hesitated before rolling his underwear down, his compliance didn't take long.

"Hands behind your back, legs apart. Next time, I expect no hesitation." Luke gave his trainee sub a critical examination. There were no tattoos or scars to mark Skye's skin and no piercings. A few freckles decorated his collarbone. Neatly trimmed dark hair bedded his cock, which stood proud and straight from his body. His balls were hairless and plump. Luke resisted the urge to lick his lips as he admired the sculpted muscle of youth. Skye was slender, still to fill out his frame, but stunning.

"You have a beautiful body." Skye's cheeks, already tinged with pink, darkened. "I want you to jack off for me."

"Sir?"

"Is there something you don't understand, Skye? I thought the order was clear."

"No, Sir. I understood. I was just…nothing. I'm sorry." Skye took his shaft in trembling fingers.

"Look at me. Maintain eye contact." Luke barely blinked, pinning Skye with his gaze. "Do you have a safe word?"

"No… No, Sir," Skye stuttered.

"You need to choose one. If you're uncomfortable with anything I ask you to do, you can use it and everything stops. For now, just use the word 'red' if you need to." Skye whimpered, but didn't respond. "This is the last time you'll come for a while. I suggest you enjoy it."

Skye gave his rigid cock two quick tugs. Gasping, he shot into his hand and the scent of his release filled the air. Watching him reach the moment of completion took Luke's breath away. He busied himself finding a packet of wipes in his desk drawer. He handed them over before standing and opening a glass-fronted bookcase. On a shelf inside were several unopened packages containing samples of bespoke chastity devices provided by a company interested in some joint promotional work with The Retreat. They were handcrafted and of the highest quality. Luke couldn't wait to see how the burnished steel would look encasing Skye's cock. He selected the model he preferred — an adjustable cage rather than a solid tube.

"You can wear this in the shower and it won't stop you going to the toilet. There are lighter versions, but I want you to know you're wearing it." He fitted the cage, relieved that his hands were steady. "It has an integral locking mechanism controlled by this Allen key." The ring encircling the base of Skye's balls closed as Luke twisted the octagonal key. "There. Perfect."

Skye gave his imprisoned cock a woeful look. "If you say so, Sir."

Luke chuckled. "Have a think about that safe word. You can dress now and take some time to unpack. The rest of the staff will be back shortly to make the final preparations for the party arriving tomorrow. You'll meet them at supper, which will be at seven in the staff dining room. Do you remember where that is?"

"I'll find it, Sir." Skye scrambled into his clothes.

"Skye."

"Yes, Sir?"

"Welcome to The Retreat."

Skye's shy smile held no doubt. "I think I'm going to like it here."

"I hope so. You've made a promising start." Skye blushed at the tiny bit of praise. He lowered his eyes. "Off you go."

Once Skye had left the office, closing the door behind him, Luke returned to his seat. A pile of paperwork awaited him, but his cock ached. He flipped open his trousers with a resigned sigh. Skye's bee-stung lips would be far preferable to his own hand, but he was training Skye, not using him for personal gratification. However tempting it might be, sex was off the menu. The Retreat had rules and Luke wasn't above them. He had to be an example to the rest of the team.

Chapter Three

As soon as he got back to his room, Skye stripped then stretched out on his bed. He stared at the cock cage for a long time before he dared to touch it. Just looking at it had the effect of making his shaft plump, then the metal rings pressed into his flesh, stopping his erection in its tracks. The frustration was delicious. Knowing that he couldn't remove the device and that Luke held the key also turned him on. *Fuck, why does this make me so horny?* He was not going to be able to forget, or ignore, the constricting metal cage. It didn't hurt, but its weight was noticeable. It was a little bit of Luke's control that he had no choice but to carry with him.

Skye climbed off the bed and explored his room. His new home was much more luxurious than he could have hoped, with a comfortable double bed and his own bathroom. Luke had told him that its most recent occupant, a houseboy called Rowan, had found love with one of The Retreat's guests. Staring at the peaceful forest view out of the window, Skye took a deep breath. He didn't dare wish for the same happy-ever-after for himself in case he cursed his chances. A small sigh of longing escaped him.

This is my chance to work out what I want from my life. I'm not going to screw it up. He'd already discovered that stern, ex-military blonds with a fondness for chastity featured at the top of his wish list. Working out how to create a chink in Luke's impenetrable armor would be his first challenge. The man's rare smiles, his undivided attention, were worth fighting for. Skye would have to find the courage from somewhere to go after what he wanted.

His stomach rumbled. Checking the time showed him he had been lost in his own thoughts for far too long. Luke would never trust him if he couldn't even manage to be on time for dinner. Traveling had made him feel grubby so he took a quick shower before dressing in comfortable jeans and a plain navy-blue T-shirt. Vanity wasn't one of his failings, but wearing dark colors did highlight his silver hair and unusual eyes. He pulled at a few stray strands, shoving them back into place. It had been five years since the incident that had contributed to his hair changing color and he found it hard to remember how he had looked when it had been its original dark brown. He sighed, the sadness still present but dulled by time. The past couldn't be changed — it was time to look to the future.

He only made two wrong turns on his way to the kitchen. The Retreat was a big house, corridors and staircases running in directions that seemed to make no sense. In the end, he followed the sound of voices and laughter and ended up in the right place. Meeting new people was not one of his favorite things so he held back, peeking through the doorway to observe the group of men gathered around an oblong oak table. Three of them were dressed in kitchen whites, the other three in casualwear similar to his own. There was no sign of Luke.

Hunger was the only thing that convinced Skye to take a few steps into the staff room. Everyone stopped talking and stared at him. He was tempted to turn around and run, thinking of a scene in *An American Werewolf in London* where a couple of hapless tourists walked into an old pub. At least there were no arcane symbols on the wall.

"Wow! You're stunning." The man that spoke had red hair, freckles and a cheeky grin.

"Hardly an appropriate way to create a new colleague, Rayne. Come on in, Skye. Take a seat and I'll introduce you to this rabble." The second speaker was tall and intimidating.

Skye sidled farther into the room. By the time he'd taken a seat, a mug of tea had been pushed in front of him. Wrapping his hands around it gave him something to do instead of making direct eye contact with anyone.

"I'm Tor Halvorsen, the chef. These two reprobates are my kitchen assistants, Benjy and Frank." Tor gestured to the two young men sitting either side of him. "I'm attempting to turn them into half-decent chefs. The idiot with the red hair and big mouth is Rayne, The Retreat's chauffeur slash mechanic slash pain in my backside."

"Hi!" Rayne waved. "Welcome. We're going to be great friends, I can tell."

"Last but not least, Fergus and Henry are our current houseboys. We don't have any single men staying next week so they'll be helping out wherever they're needed. With ten men in residence there's going to be a lot of errands to run."

"Hey."

"Hi."

Skye hoped he'd be able to remember their names. They all seemed welcoming and friendly, which was a relief. Tor had striking good looks and had to be a Dom from the way he took charge. He gave off the same commanding vibe that Luke did. Fergus and Henry were both very pretty and Rayne had a charming, if naughty personality. There was no one that Skye felt wary of — his first impressions were promising.

"Now, it's time to eat. No interrogating Skye, you lot. He's only just arrived and I'm sure this is all a bit overwhelming. You'll have plenty of time to get to know each other. You don't need his entire life history in the first ten minutes."

Skye gave Tor a grateful smile. He sipped his tea and took surreptitious glances at the group of men around the table. Tor took Benjy and Frank into the kitchen to help plate their meal. Fergus and Henry chattered away, clearly already friends. Skye caught Rayne's eye and got a wink in return. Rayne had mischief written all over him and Skye wished he had the same confidence. Apart from Tor, he guessed all the others were subs like him unless his first impressions were wrong — and that was a possibility. He knew better than to make assumptions based on the way people looked or even acted. He'd seen enough different men at The Underground to learn that much.

There was a scraping of chairs as the men remaining around the table pushed them back and stood. It took Skye a moment to catch up with what was going on because he had his back to the door.

"Good evening, Mr. Redding." The singsong chorus of greetings gave him a clue. Luke had arrived. Hurrying to catch up with what he guessed was an evening ritual, Skye shoved his chair back to stand. Luke's hands on his shoulders kept him in his seat.

"Good evening, gentlemen. Please be seated."

Luke sat at one end of the table where he would be opposite Tor when the chef returned, with Skye to his left and Rayne to his right. The chatter resumed as Tor and his assistants brought several serving dishes into the room, placing them on mats in the center of the table. Silverware was already laid out along with a tumbler at each place setting. Skye breathed in the rich aromas coming from the dishes and his stomach rumbled.

"It sounds like you're ready to appreciate Tor's cooking," Luke said. "Did you get settled in your room?"

Skye tried not to think about lying naked on his bed examining his cock cage. "Yes, thank you, Sir. It's very comfortable."

"Good. After we've eaten, there'll be a staff meeting to go over the specific requirements of next week's guests. After that, I'll see you in my office."

"Yes, Sir." Skye wondered what Luke might want with him. He hadn't yet had the chance to do anything wrong that he knew of. His worries were interrupted by the arrival of warm plates, which Benjy distributed. Tor took his seat while Benjy and Frank removed the covers from the serving dishes.

"Everyone tuck in," Tor instructed. "We don't stand on ceremony here, Skye. Especially where food is concerned."

Skye still waited his turn, letting the others take their share. Then a steady stream of dishes was sent his way. Lamb and rosemary casserole was accompanied by creamy mashed potatoes, carrots and broccoli.

"Take as much as you want," Rayne advised. "Tor's cooking is guaranteed to give you a tongue-gasm. You can also be sure that there's extra back in the kitchen just in case we're all super hungry tonight."

Skye gave him a shy smile and spooned a small helping of casserole onto his plate. "It smells wonderful." He tucked into the food and flavors exploded across his taste buds. He moaned before he realized what he was doing, gaining a few knowing chuckles from around the table.

"It's a good job we all have access to the gym and the pool here or we'd all be humungous. Not that being big is a bad thing, I can appreciate the benefits of a cuddly bear pinning me down and — "

"Rayne. Eat your food." The threat in Tor's voice was evident and Skye wondered if there was something going on between the handsome chef and the cheeky chauffeur. They'd make an interesting couple.

With the main course finished and cleared away, Skye didn't think he had room for anything else until Tor produced sticky toffee pudding for dessert. Steam rose from the glossy surface of the sponge, which had a layer of smooth, golden sauce all around it. There was extra-thick cream to go with it. Skye licked his lips in anticipation but only took a small portion.

"Are you sure that's all you want, Skye?" Frank asked.

Skye nodded. "I don't really have room, but I can't resist. This is one of my favorite puddings."

"Mine too." Frank served himself an enormous helping, slathering it in cream before tucking in with relish. "You'd be surprised how many calories you work off in a kitchen."

When he was finished, Skye pushed his dish away with a sigh. "That was one of the best meals I've had in ages."

"I'm glad you enjoyed it," Tor said. "There's no better compliment for a chef."

Frank and Benjy cleared everything away before producing fresh mugs for everyone and an enormous cafetière of coffee. Once everyone who wanted one had a drink, Luke cleared his throat and the chatter subsided.

"I just want a few words about next week's guests before you all get a good night's sleep. As you know, we have a group of ten coming in. Five couples, one of which is celebrating an anniversary. Each couple has chosen the theme for one of the five days that they are here. Tor will produce corresponding menus for the evening meals and Skye, Fergus and Henry will have specific costumes to wear each night. You'll find the clothes in your wardrobes, labeled by date."

Skye hadn't even unpacked his bags. He hadn't had a chance to look in the wardrobe yet and wondered what the costumes might be like. It sounded like the incoming guests were determined to have a good time.

"In order, the themes are sport, *Brideshead Revisited*, angels and devils, *A Midsummer Night's Dream* and a Roman slave auction. The guests are bringing their own outfits and the themes are just for the evenings. They'll use the facilities as they see fit during the day.

"I think most of you know Goran from The Underground—he'll be joining us tomorrow to run the bar and wine cellar for the duration. Skye will be providing table and room service. Fergus and Henry will run errands, refresh the rooms, clean and stock the dungeon, the gym and the pool. I want you all to preempt our guests' every wish. Now, are there any questions?"

"You didn't mention transport, Mr. Redding," Rayne said.

"Ah yes, thank you, Rayne. In addition to Rayne's usual car, we have a limo service on call and a minibus available if the whole group wants to go out together. If any of you are asked to arrange transport anywhere, please relay the requests to Rayne and he'll make appropriate arrangements.

"I'd like the kitchen staff and Skye to report for duty at six-thirty each morning, when Tor will brief you all on the menu requirements of the day and any specials available. Skye, you'll also be responsible for laying and clearing tables in the banqueting hall or anywhere else the guests wish to eat. Benjy, Frank and Tor will take it in turns to be on call for room service between midnight and six."

Skye raised his hand.

"Yes, Skye?" Luke asked.

"If someone could show me where everything I'll need is stored…"

"Of course. I should have thought about that. Tor, can you—"

"Leave him with me once we're done," Tor said. "I'll show him the ropes."

"You'll show him the table linen and the glassware," Luke growled.

Tor beamed, apparently pleased at pushing Luke's buttons. Skye glanced between them, his face heating. The last thing he wanted was to cause trouble. He wondered if hiding under the table might be an option.

Shaking his head, Luke sighed. "Let's make this the best week these guys have ever had. Any problems, you know where I am." He pushed his chair back.

"Don't forget, Skye. My office once Tor is done with you."

"Yes, Sir."

Luke made eye contact with everyone before he left the room.

"He's the dommiest Dom I've ever met," Rayne announced. "Shame he's not my type. Looks like you're his, though, Skye. Are you and he —"

"Rayne! Mouth closed or I'll stick the biggest ball gag I can find in it." Tor got up and Rayne followed his every movement. Skye conjectured the tall chef was exactly Rayne's type because he didn't seem at all fazed by Tor's threat, more eager that Tor follow through. Rayne gave an overdramatic sigh. "Guess I should go polish the car then."

"You guess right. If I had my way, you'd be doing it naked." Tor crooked his finger and beckoned Skye to follow him. Skye hid his grin as Rayne stuck his tongue out at Tor's back before blowing Skye a kiss and departing.

For the next half-hour, Skye did his best to memorize where everything was that he would need to lay the tables for various meals, from simple sandwich lunches to banqueting and parties. As they went, Tor reassured him that there was no problem with him asking questions.

"I'm well aware that you're going to have a lot on your hands for someone who's brand-new here and still finding his way around. Don't be afraid to ask. There are no stupid questions, okay? I'd much rather you asked than got into a panic about getting everything right. I don't expect perfection on the first day."

Though nervous, Skye was confident that he'd be able to manage. Working in a very busy, top-class restaurant had given him nerves of steel when it came to juggling the requirements of demanding customers. He resolved to take his time, not panic and ask questions when he needed to.

"Thank you, Mr. Halvorsen. I appreciate the tour."

"Well, I'll see you in the morning at six-thirty. It'll be your job to lay the table for the staff's breakfast, and serve it. It will be good to get your hand in with a few friendly faces and, unlike with the guests, you can give the cheeky ones a clip round the ear. Or, in Rayne's case, ask me to do it. Now, I think Mr. Redding is expecting you in his office so you'd best get along. He doesn't like to be kept waiting."

Skye didn't need to be told twice. He scurried from the kitchen to Luke's office where he found the door ajar. He raised his hand to knock.

"Come in, Skye." Skye lowered his hand, wondering how Luke had known he was there. He hadn't made much noise crossing the carpeted floor. He shrugged then pushed the door open. Luke sat behind his desk, paperwork spread out in front of him. He had on a pair of black-rimmed glasses that made him appear even sterner than usual. Skye gulped even as his cock jerked with excitement inside its metal prison. He'd always had a thing for men in glasses.

"Did Tor tell you everything you needed to know?"

"Yes, Sir. I just hope I can remember it all."

"I'm confident that you will." Luke gave Skye an intense stare. "You don't need training in how to be an excellent server, but there is plenty for you to learn if you want to be an equally good submissive."

Skye ducked his head. "Yes, Sir," he murmured.

"Lean forward and put your hands on the edge of the desk for balance."

As he was standing about a foot in front of the desk, bending over put Skye in a particularly vulnerable position. Luke rose from his chair and moved to stand behind him. "I believe that regular discipline is essential in training a submissive. Some men prefer to start the day with a reminder of who is in charge of a relationship. My preference is to end the day that way. You'll have the rest of the evening and all night to contemplate how you feel. For the purposes of your training, your discipline will consist of a single stroke of the cane. Any questions?"

"No, Sir." The words came out in a rush. Skye didn't want anything he said to stop what Luke was about to do. If it wasn't for the chastity device, Luke's words alone would have made Skye come.

"Keep still." Luke pressed close behind him, reaching around his body to undo his fly. He pulled Skye's jeans down his thighs, taking his underwear along for the ride. Skye shivered with excitement, eager to feel the kiss of the cane on his bare flesh. He craned his neck to watch as Luke fetched a flexible black cane from its resting place on a bookshelf. He didn't reprimand Skye for trying to see what was going on.

"One stroke."

There was a slight whistling sound as the cane broke a path through the air. When it struck, the bite of pain made Skye yelp. A line of fire ignited across both his arse cheeks and he desperately wanted to reach back and rub away the hurt. He kept his position, muscles clenching.

"You may pull up your clothes," Luke said after giving Skye's backside a pat. He laid the cane on his desk and resumed his seat behind it, his face betraying no emotion.

The rub of fabric against his sore skin made Skye wince. He couldn't wait to get back to his room and try to see the mark Luke had made, but Luke hadn't dismissed him so he stood still, hands clasped behind his back.

"We'll end each evening this way," Luke said. "Any punishments you earn during the day will be added to the number of strokes you receive. Have you decided on a safe word?"

"With everything that's been going on, Sir, I haven't had the chance to think about it. I'm sorry." Skye wondered if he had just earned his first punishment.

"There's no need to apologize. You've had a busy day and there's a lot to take in. I didn't give you a firm timescale. I'll expect you to have chosen the word by tomorrow evening. Now, you should try to relax and get a good night's sleep. You have to be up early in the morning and it's going to be a hectic — the first day with a new set of guests is always demanding."

There were so many thoughts buzzing around Skye's head he didn't think he'd be able to sleep at all.

"You may go, Skye. Try to find time to practice being still. It will help your focus."

"Yes, Sir." Skye left the office, pausing outside to let out the breath he'd been holding. He felt a little lightheaded and his arse ached. Luke had the effect of making all Skye's blood drain south toward his cock. Not that it did him any good — the weight of the chastity device seemed to have increased and he wondered how long it would be before Luke saw fit to release him. Shrugging, he made his way toward his room. Whether or not he ever got to come again was Luke's decision — worrying about it was a waste of energy. He had enough to be anxious about with a whole group of strangers arriving the next day as well as his new colleagues to get to know. Skye wanted to make Luke proud of him and that wouldn't happen if he dropped food into someone's lap or launched a room service order down the stairs because he was tired. He headed for his room, determined to get some rest.

Chapter Four

When he realized he'd read the same page three times without taking in a word, Luke pushed his paperwork away in disgust. He leaned back in his chair, rolling his shoulders to relieve some muscle tension. His concentration was shot to pieces and all because of one beautiful, innocent young man. Laying that single stripe across Skye's perfect skin had been the point of no return. With his mark on Skye's body, every possessive, protective gene in Luke's makeup told him that he'd never be able to let Skye go. The temptation to bend Skye even farther over his desk, to take him hard, had been difficult to resist.

He picked up the cane from where it rested on the edge of his desk and rolled it across his palm before slapping it down hard. He curled his fingers into a fist, gripping the pain.

"I wonder how you're feeling now, Skye." *I shouldn't have left him alone.* He tidied his desk then headed for his suite of rooms where he collected a tube of soothing balm. It was only a short walk to the far end of the corridor and Skye's door, to which he gave two rapid taps. Skye opened the door wearing a towel wrapped around his hips and nothing more.

"Luke...I mean, Mr. Redding. Is there something I can do for you?"

"Go and lie face down on the bed please, Skye. Remove the towel."

Skye's pretty eyes widened, but he obeyed without question. He lay with his head resting on his arms.

Luke admired the view for a few seconds before approaching the bed. "I should have taken better care of you earlier. Your first taste of discipline is not something to be dismissed lightly." Luke trailed his fingers down Skye's back to his arse. The livid red stripe across Skye's backside was hot beneath Luke's fingers. He uncapped the balm then smoothed some of the clear gel across Skye's skin.

"It feels good, Sir. Cool."

"After-care is important. I should have done this downstairs rather than invading your privacy because I felt guilty for abandoning you. I'm sorry." Luke touched for longer than he needed to, the act self-indulgent. "Fading already. I don't think you'll have a bruise, though it might be a bit sore tomorrow."

Skye twisted his head, trying to get a look. "I don't mind if it does bruise, Sir."

"You might not be so accommodating when you're on your feet all day working. Roll over. Spread your legs." Luke took the key to Skye's chastity device from his pocket. He undid the cage then removed it with care. Skye's cock hardened in seconds. "Do you want to come, Skye?" The question was superfluous, but Luke wanted to hear Skye's answer.

Skye fisted the bed clothes and whimpered. "Please, Sir." He spread his legs a little wider.

"You've done well today. I'm proud of you." Luke wrapped his fingers around Skye's erection. He rubbed his thumb over the head then dug his nail into the slit. That was all it took. Skye's back arched and his arse left the bed as he came with a hot gush into Luke's hand. Luke gave a low chuckle. "The impetuousness of youth. I don't believe I gave you permission." He still had hold of Skye's softening shaft.

"Sorry, Sir." Skye's lips were parted, his cheeks flushed. He took rapid, panting breaths. "I couldn't help it."

"No, you're not. But that's okay. This time." Luke went to the en suite where he washed his hands and dampened a flannel before returning to give Skye a quick clean-up. As soon as he was done, he refitted the chastity device and pocketed the key. "I'll leave you to get some rest now."

Skye looked shell-shocked, caught between the aftermath of his orgasm and the realization that his dick was once again imprisoned. Luke didn't wait for him to respond, just left the room, closing the door after him. He paused in the corridor and couldn't help but smile. He had plenty of material to fuel some inspiring dreams.

Being the manager of The Retreat had some benefits. Luke's suite had a sitting room as well as a large bedroom and bathroom. He had also installed a fridge to hold his stash of mineral water and a few bottles of decent white wine, the latter being an occasional indulgence. Now seemed to be a good time for a treat, so he poured himself a glass of chilled Pinot Grigio before parking his behind on the sectional couch in front of the flat screen. He caught the end of the news then surfed the channel guide until he found a documentary on rogue waves. Anything to do with the sea always caught his attention but on this occasion the footage of towering surf wasn't enough to drag his thoughts away from Skye.

He sipped his wine, enjoying the light, refreshing taste. It had been a while since he had indulged in a glass and as this would be the only one for some time, he intended to savor it. He never drank when there were guests in residence at The Retreat, needing to keep a clear head for the myriad small issues that always cropped up in the running of the business. He wondered how Skye would cope. Even though The Retreat was a less hectic environment than The Underground, clients paying a vast amount of money for their stay could be demanding. Luke resolved to keep a close eye on him, as much as he could without being obvious about it. He didn't want to come across as a mother hen or an irritating micromanager. Skye would think he wasn't trusted.

He thought about the scene in his office and Skye's willingness to submit to his control. Skye bending forward, perfect arse exposed, was a situation Luke couldn't wait to repeat. He loosened his waistband then slipped his hand into his underwear to fondle his rock-hard dick. He closed his eyes, picturing Skye's face. His fingers moved of their own volition, squeezing to the point of pain. His orgasm arrived to the accompaniment of a violent storm on the television, something that made him laugh out loud. The weather might be calmer in the New Forest, but there was a tempest of unfamiliar emotions building in Luke's head.

Sleep eluded Luke for some time, leaving him tired the following morning — ironic, considering his advice to Skye. He stuck to his routine and went for a run at five-thirty. The Retreat's grounds were large enough that he could circle the perimeter twice and get five miles in. It was rough ground, but he'd always enjoyed the challenge of cross-country and he returned muddy but content. After a quick shower, he headed for the staff dining room shortly after six-thirty. Tor was finishing his meeting in the kitchen so Luke grabbed a seat at the table and took advantage of first go at the coffee pot, which had been left in the middle of the table for any early risers. A few minutes later, Skye arrived carrying a tray loaded with cutlery.

"Oh, I'm sorry, Sir. I didn't realize you were in here." Skye ducked his head.

"Ignore me and carry on," Luke said. "I have coffee. I'm a happy man."

Skye grinned. He made efficient progress around the table before making more trips to deliver condiments and crockery. By the time he was done, Fergus, Henry and Rayne had arrived and Tor had joined them at the table. Skye cleared his throat. "Benjy and Frank will cook to order this morning, so if you would like to tell me your breakfast choices I'll get those sorted out for you."

Luke observed that Skye didn't have a notepad but stood waiting expectantly.

"I'll have two lightly poached eggs on granary toast, please." Luke put in his order first then watched as the others listed their choices.

"Thanks, everyone. I'll be back with some fresh fruit. In the meantime you'll find cereals, yoghurts and some pastries on the side."

"This is great," Rayne exclaimed. "I usually have to rummage around for food in the mornings."

"You do not, brat, but this is good practice for Skye," Tor said. "But don't get too used to it. You're here to work, not be treated like you're staying in a five-star hotel."

Rayne poked his tongue out when Tor turned away from him.

"Tor, I think Rayne would benefit from some discipline later today. Perhaps you could oblige," Luke said.

Rayne gaped. "But—"

Luke silenced his protest with a disapproving glare.

"It would be my very great pleasure," Tor said.

"Excellent."

Rayne looked from Luke to Tor then back again, mouth open. For once he didn't have a mouthy retort to hand, a miracle in itself.

Skye returned with a big dish of fresh fruit. "I've placed your orders. Is there anything else I can get for anyone?"

"Sit down and join us, Skye." Tor gave him a reassuring smile. "This lot can help themselves from now on."

Luke made eye contact with Skye then patted the chair next to him. Skye slipped into the seat with an audible sigh of relief. "You did fine," Luke said. "It's not easy, remembering everything."

"I don't have a problem with food orders," Skye said. "I've always been able to remember those. But Tor has a hundred cupboards in that kitchen then there's different places for the linen, glassware, silverware…" He sounded a bit panicked.

"Eat something, it'll make you feel better."

"I'm not sure I can," Skye said. "I'll be fine once the guests arrive and we get into the swing of things."

He did look pale, but served himself some fruit then picked at it. Luke didn't hassle him but resolved to keep an eye on how much Skye ate. He was too slim to skip meals.

Once the hot food was ready, Skye scurried in and out of the kitchen fetching plates, until everyone had their meal. Every order was one-hundred-percent accurate. Once Benjy and Frank joined them, the noise level around the table rose as everyone enjoyed breakfast and got ready for the day. Skye nibbled a piece of toast but didn't have anything else.

Luke cleared his throat to get everyone's attention. "Fergus, Henry and Skye, dress for today is black leather trousers and boots, no shirts, house collars. I want you all in the entrance hall at ten o'clock, which is when our guests are due to arrive. I'm not sure how many cars they're bringing between them, but, Rayne, be ready to move them to the garages. Goran should be here around eleven." He paused, acknowledging the various nods of understanding from around the table. Fergus and Henry were experienced subs and he had no concerns about their abilities. Rayne was a known quantity and behaved himself around the guests. Skye needed some personal attention.

"Sir, I don't have any leather trousers," Skye said, worry lines appearing around his eyes.

"You'll find a pair in your wardrobe," Luke reassured him. "Mr. Hoffman had your sizes emailed and the boys have sorted out your clothes from the stock we keep here. Everything you need related to your job will be provided."

"Thank you, Sir."

"If Tor has nothing for you to do until our guests arrive, I'd like you to join me in my office."

Rayne giggled, earning himself a glower from Tor.

"That's another two strokes added to your discipline, brat," Tor said, not sounding at all disappointed.

"I think it's time everybody got to work," Luke said.

"Would you like me to clear the table?" Skye asked, directing his question to Tor.

"Thank you for the offer, Skye but that's not necessary. It won't take a moment to put out the plates of pastries we've made to serve with hot drinks later. You go along with Luke. Once you've greeted the guests, come back here. You can relay any specific requests about lunch to me and any calls for room service will come through to the kitchen."

"He'll be here," Luke said. "Have a good day, everybody."

There was a palpable air of excitement as everyone went about their duties. Luke enjoyed the anticipation as much as anyone, though he had more to worry about. He felt responsible for each and every detail at The Retreat. Guests paid significant money for their stay and expected perfection. A never-ending pile of paperwork waited in his office and there was little else he could do for the next two hours. If he lurked near the kitchen as Tor swung into action, he risked a harder spanking than Rayne was due for. The boys wouldn't say anything, but he got under their feet if he hovered and they all knew what they were doing. He had to step back and let them get on with it.

"I stay out of the way from now until the guests arrive," Luke said to Skye, who was trailing behind him as he walked. "It's safer." As if illustrating his point, Fergus ran past, almost hidden behind a huge bunch of flowers. Luke was about to shout a reprimand but changed his mind and shook his head instead. His office provided sanctuary from the mayhem. Once he and Skye were inside, Luke closed the door, sealing them away from the outside world. "Sanctuary. Take your clothes off and don't worry, I'll make sure you have plenty of time to get ready for our guests."

It was clear from Skye's bewildered expression that he had not expected the order. He undressed anyway, a pink blush that Luke found endearing spreading across his cheeks. "Hands behind your back, legs apart." Luke walked around Skye, inspecting every inch of his body. The marks on his backside had disappeared completely. The chastity device glinted in the low light.

"Is the cage causing you any problems? Any sore spots or chafing?"

Skye shook his head. "I wouldn't call it comfortable, Sir, but it doesn't hurt."

"Good." Luke placed a cushion on the floor to the side of his chair. "Kneel on that." He waited while Skye made himself comfortable. "There's purpose behind everything I do with you, Skye. I know you're anxious about today and I want you to be as relaxed as possible. I'm going to blindfold you and, while I get some work done, I want you to focus on being as still and silent as you can be. Do you understand?"

"Yes, Sir."

"Tell me your safe word."

"Napoleon, Sir. I decided to choose a name from military history."

"Good choice. Not a name you're likely to shout in the throes of passion. At least I hope not." Skye giggled then stopped as if uncertain whether laughing was allowed. "I like to hear you laugh. I want you to enjoy your time here." Luke retrieved a leather blindfold from the stash of equipment in a box under his desk. He could have used a soft strip of cloth but had a preference for heavier materials. He buckled the blindfold around Skye's head, making sure it was correctly positioned. Skye moved his head from side to side as if attempting to see, but there was no chance any light would penetrate the thick cloth.

"I'm not going to leave you. You won't be alone for a moment and you have your safe word. Use it and this stops." Luke used a set of steel cuffs to bind Skye's hands behind his back. "Let me know if you have any tingling in your fingers."

"Yes, Sir." Skye's breathing, which had sped up, slowed again.

"Are you warm enough?"

Skye nodded so Luke sat behind his desk and began to work. Every now and again he ruffled Skye's hair but found that he was able to concentrate on future guest bookings despite the beautiful, naked submissive kneeling next to him. He tapped away on his keyboard and time passed quickly. Skye didn't make a sound. His head dipped, his muscles relaxed. Luke was sorry he had to disturb him when the time came.

"Skye, it's time for you to get ready." He stroked Skye's silver hair as he undid the blindfold. Skye blinked at him, then smiled and Luke's heart melted just a little bit. He undid the cuffs before helping Skye to stand. "How are your legs? Any pins and needles?" To his surprise, Skye leaned against him, nuzzling against his chest. "Bondage suits you, doesn't it?" He wrapped his arms around Skye's lean frame, holding him close.

"Makes me feel safe, Sir," Skye murmured. "I feel so much calmer now."

Luke ran a hand down Skye's back to cup his arse. "I'll always keep you safe." Skye's caged dick pressed against Luke's thigh. Holding him felt good and Luke had no inclination to let go, but he had to.

"Sadly, you and I have jobs to do. You have twenty minutes to change and get back down here, okay?"

Nodding, Skye pulled on his clothes. "Sorry, Sir. I didn't mean to…"

Luke pressed a finger against Skye's lips. "Hush now. You haven't done anything wrong. We'll talk about this scene tonight, before your discipline."

"Yes, Sir."

As Skye slipped out of the door, socks and boots in his hand, Luke couldn't help but smile. Skye was already getting under his skin and it wasn't an uncomfortable feeling.

Chapter Five

Skye needed a liberal amount of talcum powder to get into the leather trousers he found in his wardrobe. His first attempt, wearing underwear, had failed despite some heroic wiggling. He discarded his boxer briefs with a sigh then squirmed into the skin-tight garment by lying on the floor and pretending to be a caterpillar. Once they were on, the trousers were comfortable, the fine, supple leather molding to his body. They were low slung, so much so that the top of his treasure trail was visible, as was the outline of his caged cock.

Nobody's going to be looking at me. Skye really hoped that was true. He donned socks then laced his black leather combat boots. There was no sign of the house collar Luke had mentioned so Skye headed back downstairs to ask where he could get one. Even though there were still ten minutes before the guests were due to arrive, everyone but the kitchen crew was gathered in the entrance hall. As Skye came down the stairs, heads swiveled and several sets of eyes fixed on him.

"Bloody hell." Rayne gaped.

"He looks hotter than we do." Fergus nudged Henry, who grinned.

"He so does."

Skye stalled, not knowing whether to continue his descent or turn around and run back to his room. He met Luke's eyes, sending a silent plea for help.

"Your outfit isn't quite complete, is it, Skye? Come here, please." Luke crooked a finger. He held a strip of leather in his hand. Skye kept his gaze fixed on Luke as he tackled the rest of the stairs. He dropped to his knees in front of him because it felt like the right thing to do, ignoring the gasps from the men around him. Luke brushed his fingers down Skye's cheek before buckling the collar around his neck. He tested its fit.

"Not too tight?"

"No, Sir."

"Good. If I'm not mistaken, I think I can hear our guests arriving." Luke tapped Skye's shoulder. "Up you get. Stay close to me. You'll be fine."

Skye relaxed his hunched shoulders, glad that there was now something else to draw people's attention away from him. Rayne, Fergus and Henry dashed outside, ready to help with the luggage, and Luke followed them at a more sedate pace to stand on the front steps. Skye stayed as close to his side as he could.

Three cars, driving in convoy, pulled up in a scatter of gravel. Men spilled from every door, laughing and chattering. Skye couldn't help but smile at their exuberant excitement. He tried to work out in his head who was with who. It was clear that two older men, in their sixties he guessed, were together. They looked on with benevolent amusement as the others unloaded a growing pile of cases and bags.

"Wait here." Luke made his way toward the older couple. He shook hands with one of them and introduced himself. Skye couldn't hear their conversation, but it was clear that one man deferred to the other. He decided he should be doing something to help instead of standing around like a spare part, so he joined the procession of baggage handling and soon everything was piled in the hall, surrounded by a gaggle of guests.

"Skye," Luke said, "please take everyone through to the banqueting hall for refreshments. In the meantime, we'll get the luggage to your rooms, gentlemen. Perhaps if someone could help divide up the pile so that we know which bags belong to each of you?"

Skye ended up accompanying a group of five who, from their conversation, he guessed to be Doms. In the banqueting hall, there was a roaring fire in the grate and several groupings of comfortable chairs. Tea and coffee were already set out on the long table, along with plates of miniature pastries. Skye asked each man in turn what he would like then served him. He got a lot of kind smiles and encouraging words as if they could sense how nervous he was. He'd only just finished when the rest of the guests arrived, following Luke and speaking in excited whispers. Like homing pigeons in formation, they headed for their partners.

"May I serve the subs, Sir?" Skye asked Luke, not sure about the correct protocol.

Luke cleared his throat—all it took to silence the room. "Gentlemen, I'd like to introduce Skye, who will be your server this week." He squeezed Skye's shoulder, giving reassurance but also, Skye felt, announcing his claim. A few knowing looks were cast his way. The Oriental rug became an object of fascination. "Are you happy for Skye to talk directly to your partners or should he speak to Doms only?"

"I'm Roy," the older sub announced. "Saul and I are celebrating our fortieth anniversary together this week and we'd prefer not to stand on ceremony. We just want to have fun with our friends." He looked at his partner, who returned his smile. "I think we're very lucky to have a sweet thing like Skye looking after us and he should feel free to talk to anyone. That's right, isn't it, Sir?"

"Couldn't have put it better myself, love. After forty years together, believe me, I know who's in charge." Saul's comment got a chorus of laughter. He gave Roy's arse a gentle slap. "Perhaps it would help if we did a round of introductions?"

Skye tried his best to remember all the names but hoped that 'sir' would suffice when he forgot.

"We are delighted to have you all here," Luke said. "Please relax and enjoy yourselves. The houseboys will be back soon and will give you the grand tour in two groups to avoid crowding, then you can get settled in your rooms — and discover their secrets. Lunch will be served at your convenience, and if you have any special requests, please let Skye know so he can relay information to the kitchen. I'll leave you in Skye's capable hands, but I'll be at your disposal all week should you need anything at all."

Skye gulped and resisted the urge to grab Luke's arm to prevent him from leaving.

"You'll be fine. You can do this. I'll see you later." Luke gave Skye a rare smile before he left. Skye touched his collar, squared his shoulders then began another round of the guests, making sure all their refreshment needs were met. He even plucked up the courage to discuss lunch arrangements with Roy and Saul who were more than happy to leave all the menu choices to Tor. They seemed such a relaxed and amenable couple, comfortable in their own skins and with each other. Skye hoped that one day he'd be able to achieve the same serenity.

When Fergus and Henry arrived, there was a brief skirmish as everyone debated who should go on the tour with who, but they managed to sort themselves into one group of four and another of six before disappearing in different directions. Skye sighed, glad to have some space and relieved that he hadn't messed anything up so far. He walked through to the kitchen to fetch a trolley. Benjy and Frank were beavering away, heads down. Local radio gave them a soundtrack to work to and it made Skye giggle to see them both bop in time to some pop tune he didn't recognize. Benjy and Frank noticed him and both waved but kept working.

"They're banned from singing," Tor commented. "Neither one of them can hold a tune worth a damn. My ears don't need that kind of torture."

"I came for the trolley to clear the refreshments," Skye explained. "There are no special requests for lunch other than those you already know about from the bookings. They'd like it served around one o'clock, but buffet style is fine. They're very happy for you to sort out menus for the entire week."

"The kind of clients I love," Tor said. "A buffet is perfect. Once you've cleared, you can lay again for lunch. Use the oak sideboard for the crockery and silverware, a white cloth for the main table, and I'll need..." Tor paused, muttering the names of various dishes. "Eight mats for the hot dishes."

"Yes, Chef." Skye was glad to have clear instructions.

"Okay, you carry on. Don't worry about coming to me if you have any questions. It's only day one and I don't expect you to remember everything."

Skye cleared the banqueting hall, making sure he'd found all the various plates that had been abandoned on various surfaces, then made preparations for the lunch service with an efficiency born of experience. He only had to ask Tor once — to locate linen napkins, which had been put away in the wrong place. He took pride in doing a good job, He enjoyed service and the pleasure it gave him. The feeling of satisfaction over a well-set table was hard to beat. Sparkling glasses, gleaming silverware and pristine linens made a beautiful picture. The Retreat provided the best of everything and, though he was a little nervous about dropping an expensive glass or plate, his hands remained steady.

He had some time, so ventured outside to see if he could find some foliage to add a bit of natural colour to the table. The chill air on his skin reminded him that he had no shirt on and the sun had little warmth. He chuckled at how quickly he had got used to wearing so little. He hurried across the lawn to the nearest border, wishing he'd thought to bring some scissors. He was excited to see that there were dozens of late-blooming roses in a gorgeous shade of deep red, which would look great with some trailing ivy and a few stems of foliage. He reached for one, careful to avoid its thorns.

"What on earth do you think you're doing out here, Skye?" Skye whirled around to find Luke advancing toward him. "No, don't say anything. There can be no good reason for you being out here in the cold without a top." Luke stripped off the dark gray pullover he had on over his shirt. "Arms up." He slipped the jumper over Skye's head. It still held the warmth of Luke's body and was incredibly soft. A waft of fabric conditioner reached Skye's cold nose.

"I was getting some flowers for a table display, Sir. I didn't realize how cold it was out here." Skye wrapped his arms around his body, giving himself a comforting hug. He hated that Luke was angry with him.

Luke's expression softened. "You'll rip your hands to pieces if you try to pick those roses. Here." He pulled a Swiss army knife from his pocket. "Use this." He levered out a blade that looked like a miniature saw. "This one should do the trick."

Skye selected a dozen roses, some in bloom, some still in bud, before gathering some lengths of ivy and other foliage. Luke held out his arms so that Skye could pile everything into them, taking care not to stab him with a thorn.

"I think that's enough, Sir."

"Inside then. I need to get you warm."

Luke's concern heated Skye from the inside though his teeth were chattering. Inside, Luke walked straight through to the banqueting hall.

"Sit in one of those chairs by the fire."

"I should…"

The look Luke gave Skye left him in no doubt that if he didn't park his butt in front of the flames, it was likely to be on fire for another reason. He sank into one of the armchairs, leaning toward the heat. As his nose defrosted, it started to drip.

"Here." Luke thrust a white cotton handkerchief into Skye's hand. "Don't worry, you can keep it."

Skye blew his nose. He thawed quickly, his skin warming until he was so hot he had to move his chair back from the fireplace. He glanced at Luke from beneath his lashes.

"You and I need to have a conversation about you taking better care of yourself," Luke scolded.

"I'm sorry, Sir." Skye started to take off his borrowed jumper.

"Leave that on. You can take it off again when you're serving lunch but not before."

"Yes, Sir." Secretly, Skye was delighted that he got to keep wearing Luke's clothing even if the pullover was far too large for him.

"What am I going to do with you?"

"Spank him?" A booming voice rang out across the hall.

Skye twisted around to see who had arrived. He recognized the huge man as Goran, the barman from The Underground.

"Not a bad idea, Goran." Luke grinned then walked across the hall where he was engulfed in a bear hug. Once he had extricated himself, he shook Goran's hand. "It's good to see you. I'm afraid there's not much time for niceties. You'll need to get straight to work because there's less than an hour before lunch service, but we must catch up later."

"Sounds good. Just point me at the bar. I left my bag in the car — I can deal with it later." Goran gave Skye a wink.

"Give me your keys and I'll ask Rayne to sort it out. He can take your luggage to your room once he's parked your car around the back."

"Is Rayne the cute redhead with the motor mouth? I think I saw him pick people up from The Underground a few times." Goran handed over his keys.

"That's him."

"Hmm…another one in need of a spanking. Seems to be a common problem around here. I like it."

"In his case, you might have to join a queue."

Skye chuckled but went silent when the two Doms turned their collective attention on him. He gulped.

"Time you got back to work, Skye," Luke said. "Perhaps you could show Goran where to go — he can keep an eye on you for me. No more half-naked escapades in the grounds, okay?"

"Half-naked, eh? I'm intrigued. Seems I've been missing out on the action and there was me thinking I was in for a quiet week down here in the sticks." Laughing, Goran gave Luke's shoulder a squeeze.

"No, Sir. I mean, yes, Sir." Skye struggled out of the armchair, which was doing its best to swallow him whole. He could tell Luke was trying not to smile by the way his eyes glittered. "Have you been here before, Sir?" he asked Goran.

"Goran's good enough for me, boy, I think you already have a 'Sir'." He threw a glance at Luke. "But to answer your question, no, I haven't had the chance yet. Maybe when I have my own sub to bring with me, I'll give the place a try."

"I'll leave you to it," Luke said, heading for the door. "Behave yourself, Skye."

Skye wasn't sure whether there was a threat or a promise implicit in the order. He shook his head in an attempt to clear it.

"The bar has been set up in the snug and that's where we'll bring the group for their pre-meal drinks at lunchtime and before dinner. I'll be around to help if you need me. There are wine lists in there too. Luke printed them out, but if you need them changed, I can do that for you. It's through here." Skye walked the short distance to the snug.

"We'll encourage them to order wine while they're in here, then I can bring the bottles through once they're seated," Goran said, taking everything in. "Are there any ice buckets around here?"

Skye showed Goran the cupboard where the buckets were stashed. "It's a buffet lunch, so they may be a bit all over the place, but it will be set up in the banqueting hall where we were just now. There are loads of small tables to use for drinks. Lunch is at one, so I wouldn't be surprised if some of them start finding their way down here soon."

Goran moved behind the bar, checking things over. Skye wished he could be anywhere close to how self-assured Goran was. The big man seemed like he belonged right where he was. "Okay, Skye. I'm going to rearrange some of these bottles into an order I prefer. You can get back to whatever it was you were doing that got Luke so flustered. Well, maybe not exactly that." He laughed, making a deep rumbling sound. "Never thought I'd see the day. He must think you're something special."

Skye shrugged. "I'm not."

"Oh, sweetheart. Have you taken a look in the mirror recently? You turned heads at The Underground and I'd say you already have Luke Redding wrapped around your cute little finger."

Skye's confusion must have shown on his face.

"Such an innocent. Pay attention, Skye. Luke's training you for himself, even if he doesn't realize it yet."

"He is? How…I mean, he hasn't said anything."

"I think you should talk to him about it, not me. You trust him, don't you?"

Skye nodded.

"Well, he might not trust himself. It's as much your job to take care of him as it is his to keep you safe. I find the best subs are always the most observant. There you go—Goran's tip of the day. No charge."

Skye left Goran to his bar and went back to the roses. It didn't take him long to put together two arrangements for the main table, but his mind was elsewhere, full of thoughts of Luke. He wasn't sure Goran had it right. It was difficult to know because Luke's face gave little away. Skye resolved to follow Goran's advice and pay more attention. He could hear people approaching, so after one last look over the table, he stripped off Luke's pullover and went back to join Goran in the snug. Goran had taken off his jacket and was now clad in a leather harness that accentuated his chest. He gave Skye another wink.

"Very pretty."

"Thanks, Goran." Skye didn't think he could use the same word to describe Goran, but there were plenty of adjectives he could have found to describe those firm pecs and bulging arm muscles. He didn't get a chance, though, because the first guests weren't far behind him and soon he had no time to think about anything but drink orders and keeping a bunch of boisterous men happy.

Chapter Six

By the end of the day, Skye was dead on his feet.
Dinner had been a huge success, with Tor going to
town on the sports theme. He had even carved
individual galia melons into the shape of American
football helmets, hollowed out and stuffed with fruit
salad. Skye had enjoyed listening to the exclamations of
delight as he delivered the imaginative starters.

The group had made huge efforts with their costumes
and Skye became the unofficial photographer between
courses. His own outfit of black Lycra cycling shorts at
least made running between the kitchen, bar and
banqueting hall easy. He had to put out of his mind
how obvious his cock cage was beneath the clingy
material. Fergus and Henry only wore Speedos, so
compared to them Skye was conservative.

He and Goran had worked well together, managing
not to get under each other's feet. The delivery of food
and wine became a coordinated dance and Goran,
despite his size, proved to be light on his feet. Skye
heard almost as many complimentary adjectives

applied to the barman as to the food by several of the subs and he could understand their appreciation. Goran wasn't Skye's type, but he was impressive physically and had a gentle but certain way about him that bred confidence. He seemed able to hold a conversation with anyone, however shy, and when Skye asked him about it he said it was part of a good barman's skill set, the same as barbers and dentists. Skye had laughed at the latter, but when he thought about it, his dentist did always insist on holding a conversation even when Skye's mouth was stuffed full of instruments and his entire head numb from anesthetic.

The meal stretched out over almost three hours then everyone had moved back to the snug to be closer to the bar. Fergus and Henry had helped Skye clear the table. He'd told them it wasn't necessary because he didn't want anyone to think he wasn't capable of doing his job, but they had insisted and he'd been grateful because of the number of plates and dishes to move. It was also nice to chat to them about their day. Henry had been in the dungeon helping to demonstrate some of the equipment while Fergus had been invited to join Roy and Saul in their room. They were using the blue room, which Skye remembered had an impressive sling in the canopy of the four-poster bed. Fergus seemed to have had a great time and hoped that he would be invited back the next day.

Skye enjoyed hearing their stories, but he didn't envy them their roles. He couldn't imagine playing with a man he didn't know well, let alone a couple or a group. Fergus and Henry made their way to the snug to join the crowd and Skye made a few advanced preparations for breakfast before checking in at the kitchen where Tor was on his own, scrubbing down the work surfaces.

"Hi, Chef, is there anything else you'd like me to do?" Skye asked.

"Hey, Skye. Wasn't that a busy evening? You did really well getting all the food out so fast and I appreciate your warnings about delays between courses. Why don't you take yourself off to bed? You have an early start in the morning, though I imagine the houseboys will be up late partying, so that might reduce the numbers for staff breakfast. I already sent Benjy and Frank up to their rooms, they were exhausted."

"If you're sure, Sir. There were a lot of compliments about the food and I loved all the different ball-shaped cookies you served with the coffee."

"I can't take any credit for those — the boys came up with the idea by themselves and did all the icing work. It's nice to get good feedback, though. Once I'm done here, I'll pop into the snug to say hello. I'm on duty for room service tonight, so you can go and relax. I'll see you in the morning."

Skye looked forward to the peace and quiet of his room and his comfortable bed. He had no ambitions for anything more than a good night's sleep, snuggled beneath the covers. He had a stop to make first, though. A stop that made renewed energy sizzle through his veins.

He approached Luke's office with caution, but the door was open and Luke nowhere to be seen. Skye wondered what he should do. He was about to head upstairs when he noticed that the main door was open a crack. He gave it a tentative push and found Luke standing on the front steps, staring out into the rain. He turned and for a moment Skye fancied that his eyes lit up.

"I'm sorry, Sir, I didn't mean to disturb you, but Tor has finished with me for the day and I wasn't sure…"

"You're not disturbing me, Skye." Luke beckoned him forward. "I was just getting a breath of fresh air after a day inside. I love this time of year. The beginning of autumn smells different somehow." He frowned. "You shouldn't be out here without a shirt on. I think we've discussed this once today already."

Skye had completely forgotten how little he was wearing. "I'm not cold, Sir. I didn't even realize it was raining."

"You're shivering." Luke ran his hand down Skye's bare arm. "If it's not from the cold, what's making you nervous?"

With every atom of his being Skye craved more contact, to be wrapped in the security of Luke's embrace. He ducked his head, afraid to give away his need.

"Well, I think we should find somewhere a little warmer for your evening discipline." Luke took Skye's hand and led him inside. Skye expected to be taken into Luke's office, but instead Luke took him upstairs to the staff accommodation wing. "One of the advantages of being manager of this place is the suite of rooms that comes with the job," Luke said as he opened his door and led Skye inside. "There's a bit more space to maneuver in here than there is in my office."

They stood in the expansive but cozy lounge. Skye's gaze was drawn to an open door on the far side of the room through which he could see the corner of the bed. He pinched his lower lip between his teeth, seeking the distraction of a small bite of pain.

"Take your clothes off, Skye."

There was a slight delay while his brain processed the order, but it took seconds to kick off his trainers and rolled down the cycling shorts. Skye stood, clad only in chastity cage and collar, in front of the only man he'd ever contemplated belonging to. He clasped his hands behind his back to stop them shaking and in its metal prison, his dick attempted to harden.

"You've earned a punishment today, Skye. For not looking after yourself. That's not acceptable." Luke took a seat in one of the armchairs. "Over my lap, please."

Heat flooded Skye's cheeks, but he took the few short steps needed to reach Luke's knee. Getting into position was nothing like how he had imagined. There was no grace involved and only Luke's hand on the small of his back kept him in place instead of tipping head first onto the carpet. Blood rushed to his head, which dangled near the floor between his arms. His toes still touched the ground but not enough to steady him. His caged cock nestled between Luke's parted thighs.

"Six." Luke accompanied the word with the first blow. The contact with Skye's backside shocked Skye into a yelp. Heat seared his buttocks. Luke spanked him six times in rapid succession and, when he was done, he rested his hand across Skye's backside while Skye took heaving breaths.

"Up you get." Luke helped Skye get upright then patted his lap. Skye straddled his thighs, facing him. "Look at me."

Skye had to force himself to meet Luke's gaze, expecting to see disappointment. Instead, Luke smiled.

"You took your punishment with grace. That replaces your discipline for tonight." In his hand he had the key to Skye's chastity device and it was the work of a moment for him to remove it. Skye held his breath as his cock attempted to beat the world record for getting hard. The need to come was painful. He shifted and the movement reminded him that he'd just been spanked.

"The pain makes you want to come even more, doesn't it?" Luke wrapped his hand around Skye's shaft. Skye froze, knowing that even the slightest friction would trigger an orgasm he was unable to control. "Hands behind your back."

Skye gripped his left wrist with his right hand, digging his fingers in hard. Luke increased the pressure of his grip.

"Please..." Skye took rapid, uneven breaths.

For a few painful seconds, Luke didn't move. Then he reached between Skye's legs and pressed the area behind his balls. Skye came in a rush of heat and joy, the speed of his orgasm frightening in its intensity. His entire body shook and when he was done he collapsed against Luke's chest, sobbing.

Luke stroked his back, whispering calming words into his ear. Skye didn't want to move but guessed that he should, so he pulled back a little.

"Where do you think you're going? Swing your legs around so you can get more comfortable."

Skye found himself nestled in Luke's lap, his head resting against Luke's chest. He could feel the beat of Luke's heart. "What about you, Sir?" Skye whispered.

"If I want you to do something for me, Skye, I'll tell you. Now stop worrying and relax. How did you find the scene in my office earlier today? Was there anything about it that worried you?"

"Only how much I enjoyed it, Sir. It's hard to describe how I felt afterward—less scattered, more…centered."

"That's what I intended, so I'm pleased. I'll try to give you some quiet time each day, though it might not always be possible."

"Yes, Sir. That sounds good." Luke was warm and strong and safe. Skye sighed and pressed closer. Luke stroked his hair. He didn't attempt further conversation, but the silence wasn't uncomfortable and Skye soon drifted into a doze. When Luke stood, picking Skye up, Skye was aware of what was happening but not fully conscious. Luke carried him down the corridor to Skye's room where he tucked him into bed and gave him a soft kiss on the cheek before he left, closing the door behind him. Skye curled into a ball, knowing that he would dream about spankings and Luke, his aching arse assured him of that.

* * * *

Skye awoke with a start, his hand wrapped around his softening shaft. Sticky fluid coated his fingers and he fought to remember whatever dream had caused his reaction. He could only recall vague images of Luke's face, nothing more.

He groped for his clock, worried that he might have overslept and missed the alarm, but there were still fifteen minutes before he needed to get up. He was wide awake so he took a long, hot shower, taking the time to shave his groin. It was fantastic to be free of the chastity device, but if Luke chose to lock him up again, he didn't want hair getting in the way. He hoped Luke would approve, then wondered if he should have waited for permission first.

You're never happy unless you've got something to worry about, idiot. Berating himself didn't help much. He hadn't had permission to come in his sleep either but hoped that was a forgivable offense. He pulled on underwear, a comfortable pair of jeans and a soft sweater that his grandmother had given him the previous Christmas. Its deep shade of purple brought out the color of his eyes. Socks and plain black trainers completed the outfit. No doubt there would be instructions as to what he should wear for the rest of the day, but for now, casual clothes would do to serve the staff breakfast.

When he got downstairs, Benjy and Frank were already hard at work in the kitchen, Benjy prepping vegetables and Frank peeling a mountain of potatoes. They both paused to wave when Skye stuck his head around the door.

"Morning. Big roast for the *Brideshead* theme tonight, so we're getting ahead while we can," Frank announced.

Tor emerged from the walk-in refrigerator, carrying a massive side of beef on a platter.

"Nice to see you're up promptly, Skye. You can go ahead and lay for the staff breakfast if you would."

Skye nodded and got to work, pleased that he remembered where everything was and didn't have to ask. Tor came in with the coffee pot in one hand and a jug of freshly squeezed juice in the other. He put them down on the table.

"You won't know this, Skye, because I think you had already gone to bed, but the boys agreed last night that they would take the entire group out in the minibus for a tour of the forest today. We are putting together packed lunches for everyone, so you'll be able to take a break for part of the day at least. Rayne, Fergus and Henry will be going with them. It's a great plan because we have a real feast planned for tonight and this will make it much easier to get everything ready. You'll need to polish the banqueting silverware and get out all the best china. Think National Trust stately home."

"Is there anything else I can do to help?" Skye asked.

"Just put everything out for breakfast. We won't be cooking to order for the staff this morning but there are croissants and some *pains au chocolat* warming. You'll find some Greek yogurt and honey in the fridge and some bowls of melon balls, which we made from fruit left over from yesterday's dinner."

Skye got everything onto the table before the others arrived—Benjy and Frank bleary-eyed but hungry, Rayne bright-eyed and chatty. Luke came in last, but there was none of the chair-scraping ceremony of the previous evening. Only Goran was absent.

Soon they were all settled and eating. Skye was surprised at how comfortable he felt in the company of men he'd only known for a short time, but the atmosphere was relaxed and easy. He stole frequent glances at Luke, who had his head buried in the newspaper, his spectacles balanced on the end of his nose. Just watching him made Skye hard and when Luke peered at him over the top of the paper, Skye didn't know where to look. If Luke found Skye's discomfiture amusing, it didn't show. He folded his newspaper, leaving it next to his plate while he helped himself to a second croissant.

"These are delicious, Tor. As good as any from a French *boulangerie*."

"Frank's work," Tor said. "He has some talent for pastry."

Frank blushed bright red. Skye guessed that Tor didn't hand out praise often but when he did, it meant something. He reacted the same way if he got even a hint of approval from Luke.

"Any time you feel like practicing, Frank, I'd be happy to be your taste tester," Rayne said. "I mean, I know I'd be taking a serious risk but for you, I'd be willing to expose my taste buds to danger."

Frank threw his balled-up napkin at Rayne's head.

"Did you not learn your lesson yesterday, brat?" Tor growled.

Rayne blinked, all innocence. "Who, me, Sir? I don't know what you mean."

"I think you need to up your game, Tor," Luke said, hiding a smile. "I have to admit I am somewhat surprised that Rayne isn't carrying a cushion around with him today. You must've gone far too easy on him."

There were muted chuckles from around the table.

"Something I will have to remedy later on today," Tor said, scowling. "Benjy, Frank, enough loafing around. Get your backsides into the kitchen. You've got work to do."

Rayne pushed his chair back. "I'll bring the minibus around to the front of the house ready for today's trip." He swallowed the last of his coffee. "See you later, Chef."

Skye watched with interest. The sizzle of attraction between Rayne and Tor was obvious. Tor shook his head then headed for the kitchen, muttering under his breath about brats in need of discipline.

"Fergus. Henry. Time you were doing whatever it is you need to do to keep yourselves out of mischief until the group is ready to go. I'm sure you both have plenty to get on with." Luke managed to sound threatening without ever raising his voice.

Fergus and Henry scuttled out of the room leaving Luke and Skye at the table.

"If you're all finished, Sir, I'll clear away," Skye said.

"Carry on. I need to get to work too. But once you're done with the guests' breakfast, come and find me."

"Yes, Sir." Skye was desperate to find out more about Luke's plans for the day but didn't dare ask and Luke left the kitchen shortly afterward so he lost his chance. He cleared quickly, stacking the dishwasher and switching it on before heading to the banqueting hall to get everything ready for the guests. They arrived in dribs and drabs, making it easy to keep up with service and Skye was brave enough to join in the conversation about their plans for the day. He hoped he'd get the chance to explore the area when he had some time off. He had to fetch extra coffee three times and there were definitely a few sore heads amongst the group, but the quieter ones soon revived once they were caffeinated and full of Tor's delicious cooking.

Benjy poked his head around the door and called Skye over. "Can you give me a hand with the coolers? There are too many for me to carry on my own. Packed lunches for thirteen people take up more space than you might think."

"Sure." Skye followed him back to the kitchen then helped by heaving two of the four enormous coolers out to the front of the building, where Rayne was waiting with the minibus. After they had loaded everything up, Skye chatted with Rayne for a few minutes.

"You know, I'm sure no one would mind if you came along with us," Rayne said. "Fergus and Henry are allowed."

"Oh, it's okay. I'll be helping Tor with the preparations for tonight's *Brideshead* feast. There's loads to do."

"And you'd rather be anywhere else than stuck in a small space with so many people." Rayne patted Skye's shoulder. "You find it hard being in a crowd, don't you?"

Skye nodded. "Is it that obvious?"

"You hide it well around the guests, but I know lots of introverts. Enough to recognize the signs anyway. You ever need a quiet place to hide away, there's a workshop at the back of the garage with a small apartment over it—used to be where the chauffeur lived years ago. It has power, old armchairs, a fridge. No one will find you in there. Well, Luke would. He knows everything. Sees everything. And he keeps encouraging Tor to spank me, what's that about?"

"You love it," Skye said, laughing. "And I think Tor enjoys doing it."

"Who wouldn't?" Rayne wiggled his butt. "I have a very cute behind."

The guests started to filter outside, so Skye slipped away. He could deal with a few hours' peace and quiet, but he still called in at the kitchen to see if there was anything Tor needed him to do.

"Not for now," Tor said. "You'll find Luke in the snug with Goran. I suggest you check in with them. There will be a light lunch to serve around one for those of us that are left here, so I'd appreciate you getting back here at twelve-thirty."

"Yes, Mr. Halvorsen." Skye made his way to the snug where he found Goran and Luke sitting together at one of the low tables, discussing requirements for a drinks order. Goran gave him a wink and a smile. Luke, as always, was more serious. He pointed to a spot on the floor to one side of his chair. Skye walked across to him then sank to his knees, staying silent.

"Okay, if you think that's everything, Goran, I'll put this order in today for delivery tomorrow. Are you sure that two extra cases of champagne will be enough for Friday?"

Goran's brow furrowed. "Another one won't hurt. It's not as if it will go off. If we don't use it for this group, it'll be there for the next one. Oh, and the store is quite low on nuts for bar nibbles. Could you get in one of those mixed boxes?"

"Sure. I'll also get Tor to add some more lemons and limes to his fresh produce order and ask him to check the ice supplies, but I'm pretty sure we still have plenty of that."

"Great. I'm going to spend some time rearranging things in here a bit, then Henry and Fergus left me some orders for drinks to be left in the rooms, so I'll deal with them and make sure their ice buckets are replenished. I thought it would be nice to serve some mulled cider when the group gets back. Perhaps Skye could help me sort out trays and glasses later on?"

"Certainly. The group are due back at three, though Rayne will call if they are delayed for any reason."

"Great. That'll give me time for a nap after lunch. It was a late night last night and I didn't sleep that well."

"I hope you're comfortable in your room," Luke said. "If there's anything you need, you should talk to Fergus or Henry."

"The room is great. I'm always the same the first night away in a new place," Goran said. "I'll sleep like a baby tonight, don't worry."

Skye got a sudden picture in his head of Goran snuggled under his duvet, cuddling a pillow, teddy bear next to him. He couldn't stop himself from giggling.

"You wanted to make a contribution to this conversation, Skye?" Luke asked.

"No, Sir. Sorry."

"Hmm... I think you and I should spend some quality time together discussing the appropriate behavior of a submissive when in the company of two Dominants."

"Yes, Sir," Skye murmured.

"When does Tor need you next?"

"At twelve-thirty, Sir."

Luke checked his watch. "Then that gives us an hour for some training. Goran, are we all done here?"

"We sure are. Have fun, boys."

Luke rolled his eyes. "If you need me, I'll be in the dungeon."

Skye took a deep breath. It would only be for an hour, but the thought of spending time alone with Luke, alongside all the possibilities the dungeon offered, made his skin tingle and his cock stiffen.

Chapter Seven

It was a few degrees cooler underground, but the temperature wasn't uncomfortable—two large space heaters took care of that. Skye tried to take everything in without making his curiosity obvious. He had been intrigued when Luke had first shown him around the dungeon, but now he was about to get up close and personal with the equipment, his pulse pounded.

"Feel free to look around," Luke said. "I don't have a problem with you being curious. Have you ever used any of this dungeon furniture before, at The Underground perhaps?"

"No, Sir." Skye had seen the club's playrooms but never ventured inside. They stood in a large space with a flagged floor and stone walls. Light was provided by two bare bulbs strung on cables across the ceiling. A leather-padded cross stood in one corner, and a cage sat next to the back wall. It was large enough for a man to stand or sit in but not lie down. In the center of the room, a spanking bench with various movable sections took center stage. There were also three further doors leading from the main space, each with a small barred window set into it.

"This house has a long and interesting history," Luke said, as he walked across to one of the barred doors. "These cells have housed prisoners across the ages. We're going to use one of them." Luke opened the central door and gestured for Skye to go inside. The only equipment in the room was a reclining chair of the kind that might be found at a dentist's, complete with various instruments on moveable arms and an overhead lamp.

Skye gulped. "I've always been a bit phobic about going to the dentist. It makes me think of that scene in *Little Shop of Horrors*."

"If it helps," Luke said, "think of it as a gynecologist's chair rather than a dentist's."

"If that was your idea of humor, Sir, it wasn't funny." Skye's palms were clammy and his erection had deflated.

"It wasn't meant to be." Luke made a few adjustments to the settings of the chair, lowering a set of stirrups. "The relationship between a Dominant and his submissive is about trust and that's something that has to be earned. You have your safe word and I'll respect it. Most Dominants require that you give them full access to your body, for pleasure and for pain. I'd say it's the ultimate act of trust to hand your wellbeing over to another man."

Skye wasn't interested in what most Doms wanted — he was interested in Luke's requirements of a sub. He had no problem trusting that Luke would respect his safe word, but psychologically the piece of equipment in front of him scared him.

"Strip."

Each piece of clothing that Skye removed made him feel more vulnerable. It wasn't just the exposure of his bare flesh, or that Luke remained fully dressed — it was the act in itself. Obeying Luke's order was an act of submission.

"The color of that pullover suits you," Luke said as Skye pulled it over his head. It was such an inane comment considering the situation that Skye wanted to laugh. It made him happy to think that Luke took an interest in what he wore and how he looked when on the surface Luke could come across as cool and detached. Skye finished removing his clothes and placed them in a neat pile in one corner of the cell.

"Onto the chair."

The leather beneath Skye's arse and back was cold, but warmed quickly. His position, not quite horizontal, gave him a whole new perspective on the room and the equipment surrounding him.

"Put your feet in the stirrups."

His legs must have gained weight in the last few minutes, because they resisted Skye's attempt to lift them into position. He took a couple of deep breaths and tried again. This time he managed it and Luke's smile was reward in itself. Skye tried to stay calm as Luke buckled leather straps around his ankles so there was no way he could lower his legs again. He rotated a handle at the side of the chair and Skye's legs moved farther apart, to such an extent that he could feel the strain on his inner thigh muscles. Next, Luke fastened a wide strap around Skye's waist. The bondage helped Skye relax a little and his cock began to show interest again. A strap around each wrist linked to rails on either side of the chair rendered him even more immobile. He could lift his head and shoulders a few inches, but that was it. Even that became impossible when Luke used another handle to lower the top portion of the chair, tilting Skye's head back. A final strap went around his forehead ensuring that he could no longer see what Luke was doing.

"How are you feeling?" Luke's voice sounded from somewhere near Skye's feet.

"Nervous, Sir. Excited." Turned on. Skye kept that last thought to himself, though he guessed his straining erection made it obvious. The caress of a shift in the air brushed the head of his cock and he whimpered.

"I can keep you here like this, exposed to my view, aching to come, for as long as I want to."

"Yes, Sir." Getting the words out took effort.

"You shaved." Luke brushed a finger across Skye's belly.

"Yes…I…the cage, well it can get itchy, Sir. I hope you don't mind."

"I don't, though next time I'll shave you myself. You have to be a contortionist to do it yourself and I'd rather you didn't nick anything important. Do you miss being in chastity?"

Skye wasn't sure how to answer. He didn't want to risk losing the opportunity to come, but he did miss the weight of the cage. In his head it was like having Luke's fist wrapped around his dick.

"The truth, please. Nothing you say will change the course of the day. What happens next is my decision and I won't be swayed by how you answer."

"I do miss it, Sir. I don't understand why, but I do. I don't enjoy it but…"

"You feel safer when the ability to choose is taken away from you."

"Yes!" *How does he know that? It's like he's in my head.*

"When coming isn't an option, you don't have to worry about disobedience. Whereas now…when you don't have my permission to come, I imagine there's not much room in your head for anything else."

As Luke hadn't asked a question, Skye hoped he wasn't required to answer.

"I'm going to put a cock ring on you."

"Oh God, Sir, if you touch me…I don't think, I mean I can't…please…" Skye pulled against the straps holding him down. His safe word sat on the tip of his tongue, but he didn't want the scene to end.

"Good boy. You should always be honest with me."

"I…I came last night. I didn't mean to—it happened in my sleep. I should have told you."

"You've told me now and that's what counts. You can't help your dreams, but I think you'll be sleeping in chastity from now on."

There was a brief silence then Skye's cock was engulfed in wet heat. He couldn't comprehend what was happening at first, then Luke sucked the head of Skye's aching dick. In his wildest dreams he had never imagined that a Dom might do what Luke was currently doing. Skye screamed as he came, unable to do anything but shake in his bonds as his cock pulsed, sending his release into Luke's throat. Luke kept sucking and licking until Skye thought he would black out. Everything was too much. Too sensitive. Too overwhelming. He sobbed when Luke finally pulled away.

"Don't try to speak." Luke stroked his cheek with the backs of his fingers. "I told you there was nothing you could do to alter the course of events, didn't I?"

Skye reeled, giddy despite being horizontal.

"Now, I'm going to make sure you're thinking of me for the rest of the day."

Luke's touch as he fastened a cock ring in place was almost unbearable. Skye shuddered at the constriction but was distracted by a brush against his belly.

"What's that, Sir?"

"You'll find out soon enough." Luke unfastened the strap around Skye waist, replacing it with a narrower belt, which he passed beneath Skye's body. "This is a harness. There's a strap linking the cock ring to the belt, then another that passes between your legs to attach to the belt at the back. It will hold the plug in place."

Skye tried to process the sensation of leather against skin and the tug of the cock ring. "Wait...plug?"

"Yes. This harness is designed to hold in a plug."

Skye gasped as Luke pressed a lubed finger against his hole. He tried to bring his legs together but couldn't move them. When Luke's finger penetrated his channel, Skye's vision blurred.

"The plug isn't big — we'll work up to something larger over time." Luke moved his finger from side to side before withdrawing. Something harder and colder replaced it. "Let it in, Skye."

Skye took a deep breath as Luke pushed the plug inside him. There was a slight burn that soon faded and he could feel the stretch as a bulge on the toy made his breath hitch. Once it was fully seated, Luke passed another leather strap between his legs, nudging him to lift his arse from the chair. The strap was a snug fit between his butt cheeks and when Luke fastened it to the belt, it seemed to push the plug deeper as well as increase the pull on the cock ring.

"Good. I'll check the fit in a moment."

Skye lay boneless and limp as Luke released him from bondage and lowered the stirrups. Luke had to help him up then steady him once he was standing because his legs didn't seem to work anymore.

"I don't want you to get cold—let's get you dressed." Skye remained compliant as Luke helped him into his clothes. "It can be difficult for someone who hasn't had much practice to keep a plug in. Your body's instinct will be to push the invader out, so the harness will prevent that. The cock ring won't stop you getting an erection, but it will make it much more difficult to come. Not impossible—but you don't have my permission, so I expect you to resist."

Every time he moved, the plug shifted in Skye's channel, nudging his prostate. He shivered. "Hold me, Sir?"

Luke gathered him into a hug, wrapping both arms around him. His erection pressed into Skye's belly but Skye knew better than to say anything. It was gratifying to know that Luke had been turned on by the scene as much as Skye had been. Skye wished he could do something about it. He could imagine nothing better than sinking to his knees, releasing Luke's dick then giving it the attention it deserved. His mouth watered at the thought and he whimpered.

"You'll get used to it," Luke said. "If it gets too much, you come to me and we'll talk about it. You are not to take it off yourself."

Skye wanted to laugh at Luke's misinterpretation of his distress. "It's not locked, Sir?"

"Only by my word. I trust that will be enough." It was a statement rather than a question. Skye wished he could be so confident.

"I'll do my best, Sir. I promise."

"And that's all I ask." Luke gave Skye's arse a pat, jostling the plug and Skye caught a rare, mischievous smile.

"That's naughty, Sir."

"It is, isn't it? Now, I think it's time you got back to work. You know what you're doing?" He took Skye's hand then led him up the steps to the main house.

"Yes, Sir. Staff lunch service first, then setting up for the guests when they get back from their outing. Goran wants some helps serving drinks too."

"Are you looking forward to the *Brideshead Revisited* theme this evening?"

"I've seen both versions of the film and read the book. I can't wait to see everyone's costumes."

"They'll be spectacular, I'm sure."

The tone of Luke's voice told Skye that Luke knew something he didn't. He wondered what his costume for the night might be. Somehow, he suspected that it wouldn't be a full dinner jacket and dress trousers. He wouldn't be surprised if he ended up in the harness, a bow tie and nothing else.

* * * *

Luke kept a close eye on Skye over the course of a relaxed, casual staff lunch. The short scene in the dungeon had been intense and he was acutely aware of how new Skye was to everything. Making him wear the harness was a calculated risk, but Luke was convinced that Skye needed a permanent connection to his Dom, whether that be through a chastity cage, a plug or a collar. The more intimate the contact, the better. Skye was a bright, thoughtful young man who replayed in his head everything he experienced, but expressing his feelings didn't come easily. They had to be teased out. He had been too nervous in the dungeon to reach sub space, but the experience would still have affected him on a subconscious level. Luke wanted to be there for him if he needed to talk or wanted reassurance.

Goran held court, telling funny stories about life behind the bar at The Underground. He had an endless supply of tales about a sub called Olly who Luke learned Skye had never met, but had heard about from Alistair and Christian—two subs who had befriended him. Luke couldn't imagine Skye ever being confident enough to misbehave the way Olly did, but it was amusing to watch as he stared, open-mouthed while Goran recounted how Olly had smuggled an extra-large bag of M&Ms into the club one night, then dropped them all over the dance floor when the bag split. His Dom had made him pick them all up, crawling on his hands and knees, then given him a spanking in front of any club members who cared to watch—which was most of them.

"The trouble is, all Olly has to do is pout and bat his lashes for Joe to forgive him. They usually end up in a private room and Olly is always grinning when they emerge," Goran finished, chuckling. "That boy is a consummate brat, but there's not a bad bone in his body. He's as sweet as all the sugar he eats."

"Don't be getting any ideas," Luke said, directing his comment at Skye.

"No, Sir." Skye's lower lip was getting some abuse. He shifted in his chair and a small gasp escaped. Goran gave Luke a knowing look.

Benjy and Frank started giggling, which resulted in Tor grabbing their ears and dragging them back to the kitchen. Skye cleared the table, moving slower than usual. Goran leaned back in his chair, arms folded across his chest.

"It's his first time with a plug, isn't it?"

Luke nodded. "Just watching him move around is a challenge to my self-control."

"He is delicious. The perfect combination of innocence and submission. He's a natural. You're a lucky man, Luke."

Luke checked that Skye was out of earshot before he answered. "I'm just training him. He's not mine."

"Isn't he? Because the young man I'm looking at is at least halfway in love with you already."

"That's not possible. We've only known each other a few days and he knows I'm training him. Why would he feel anything deeper?"

"You need to talk to Joe Dexter if you want a proper answer to that kind of question. He's a psychologist."

Luke grunted. "And you're a barman. Next best thing." He pushed his chair back. "Walk with me to my office? There are a lot of flapping ears in the vicinity."

"Sure. We have time to take a turn around the grounds if you don't mind some fresh air. Be doing me a favor because I think our group are going to get rowdy tonight and I won't get another chance for a break once they're back."

"Clearing my head might be a good idea," Luke said. He led the way outside. Autumn sunshine was making a brave attempt to break through the clouds, sending shafts of light through the trees, turning the leaves to gold and copper. Luke took a deep breath of the crisp air.

"I feel more awake already."

"It's deceiving," Goran said. "It looks sunny and bright, but it's cold."

"I can't believe we've already resorted to talking about the weather," Luke said.

"We're British—it's the law."

"So now we've done our patriotic duty, where on earth do you get the impression that Skye is in love with me?" Leaves crunched underfoot as Luke strolled across the lawn, Goran at his side.

"You're probably too close to the lad to see it, but it's apparent in every look, every gesture. When you're in the room, he's a totally different person. Less shy and reserved, more confident with his place in the world."

"I can't believe I haven't spotted this myself." Luke stared the distant trees. A bird of prey he couldn't identify swept toward the ground, talons extended. Not wanting to know whether he was witnessing the death of a small furry mammal, Luke turned away.

"There's a soft heart beating beneath that cold exterior. He's getting under your skin, admit it."

"Maybe. There's something about him, something vulnerable. But he has an inner strength that I envy."

Goran didn't say anything. He didn't have to. They continued their circuit of the building in contemplative silence and Luke was grateful for the opportunity to think. He needed to be more observant. Goran had caught on in seconds to something he should have seen himself. How would he ever earn Skye's trust if he failed to read his responses? He was still deep in contemplation when they arrived back at the main door.

"Plenty of food for thought, eh?" Goran nudged him, which, from a man of his size, sent Luke sidestepping through the gravel. "Now, wish me luck because I need to invade Tor's kitchen to create my secret recipe mulled cider."

"He has a large collection of cleavers, just so you know," Luke said. "Rather you than me."

Goran's guffaw echoed around the entrance hall as they went back inside. "Well, if you're short one barman later on today, check the biggest crockpot first, okay?" He ambled in the direction of the kitchen while Luke sought the sanctuary of his office. He still had more thinking to do.

Chapter Eight

Luke emerged from his office just as the guests returned from their day trip. They spilled into the entrance hall, accompanied by a blast of cold air. Fergus and Henry immediately went about collecting coats and scarves as they were shed.

"Gentlemen," Luke raised his voice just enough to be heard over the excited chatter. "Please head for the snug where Goran has a treat for you." That caused an immediate stampede and more laughter.

"I take it the trip went well?" Luke asked in the general direction of his two houseboys who were struggling under their respective piles of clothing.

"It was brilliant, Sir. Rayne had researched all the best places to go. We saw loads of cute ponies and even had time to explore some antique shops. There was this amazing tea room in an old chapel full of second-hand books where we all had drinks." Fergus paused for breath and Henry took over.

"The two old ladies working there made fantastic hot chocolate, with marshmallows and whipped cream and sprinkles, Sir. Then Rayne took us to this picturesque ruin in the forest for our picnic lunch and Tor had packed the most amazing food." He giggled. "Then everyone was talking about the various ways they were going to work off all the calories they'd consumed. Some of these guys are really inventive, Sir." He blinked, a light blush staining his cheeks.

"I'm glad it went well. Leave all those coats and things on the banister and take yourselves through to the snug for a hot drink. I'll sort this lot out."

"Are you sure, Sir?"

"Was my instruction unclear in any way?" Luke held back a smile as the two young men scurried away in the direction of the snug.

Luke hung all the coats on two stands in the hall before heading to the snug himself. Long before he got there, the aroma of mulling spices and warm cider filled the air. It was the perfect scent of autumn. Skye hovered close to the door, tray in hand loaded with glass goblets full of steaming amber liquid. Luke went to stand next to him, surveying the room full of people who stood or sat all over the place. Goran had jugs of cider on the bar and was topping up everyone's glasses as soon as they were in any danger of nearing empty.

"Would you like a drink, Sir?" Skye asked, his tone soft as usual.

"Thanks, Skye, but I avoid alcohol when there are guests staying."

"Oh, this is the virgin version. Probably why it's not so popular. It's warm spiced apple juice."

"Well, in that case I will take one. It smells absolutely delicious. Do you know what Goran put in it?" Luke took the glass that Skye handed to him.

"I'm afraid not, Sir. He said it was a secret recipe, but there was a lot of cursing coming from the kitchen. I don't think Tor appreciated Goran rummaging around in his spice cupboard. I was a bit worried it was going to get violent in there." His bewildered expression was comical.

"Tor is very protective of his ingredients. Goran is a braver man than I am. I'm surprised he got out of there unscathed."

"He left Tor and the boys with a jug of their own. I think that did the trick."

"It's definitely going down well." Luke made his way into the melee to mingle a little. He didn't want to leave Skye's side, but the guests came first. It was gratifying to hear how much they had enjoyed their day out and the general appreciation for the attention to detail that everyone at The Retreat was going to on their behalf. Satisfied that there were no problems or issues for him to deal with, Luke retreated to the door.

"I imagine setting up tonight's banquet is going to take some time," he said, wanting to engage Skye in more conversation. Skye still remained near the door as if he wanted to be close to the exit should the crowd get too much for him.

"I'm really looking forward to it, Sir. The table is going to look magnificent and it's my first chance to use the antique silver and those big candelabra. The table decorations you ordered arrived earlier and they're absolutely beautiful. I can't wait to see the finished effect."

Luke smiled at his enthusiasm. "You must come and tell me when it's ready so that I can take a look. If you do as good a job as I think you will, I'll take some pictures for the website."

"You will?" Skye's eyes widened, glass rattling against metal as his trembling hands made the tray shake. Luke took it from him before the last two drinks could take flight. He carried it over to the bar, waving to get Goran's attention.

"Are you done with Skye? I think he needs some space."

"Sure. He's been a great help. Say thanks for me, won't you?"

Luke nodded and headed back to the door where Skye was doing his best to hide, standing half in and half out of the room.

"Goran has set you free with his thanks — why don't we go find somewhere quieter?"

Skye heaved a sigh of relief. "I'd like that, Sir."

"It's cold outside. Let's go to the staff dining room. I'm sure Tor will rustle up a pot of tea and a slice of cake if we ask nicely."

As they walked toward the kitchen, Skye's arm brushed against Luke's. Luke couldn't resist taking his hand. Skye's slender fingers were meant to nestle against his palm. It was only a short walk to the staff room and Luke found that he was loath to let go of Skye's hand, but it was necessary to pull a chair out for him and make sure he was seated comfortably. Before he could venture into the kitchen, Tor appeared in the doorway.

"I thought I heard someone come in. How about I get one of the boys to make a pot of tea?"

"That would be great, thanks, Tor. We don't want to get in your way. I know how busy you must be in there. Everything smells incredible, by the way."

"Thanks. The day trip for the guests was a godsend. Everything's well organized. There should even be time for the boys to have a short break before service starts. We're just putting the finishing touches on everything that can be prepared in advance. Then there'll be the usual last-minute chaos, no doubt." He grinned, eyes shining.

"You're an adrenaline junkie," Luke said. "Not quite the same as the battlefield, is it?"

"Not quite, but I appreciate the lack of bullets flying around the place."

Skye looked between them, mouth open. Tor gave him a wink before disappearing back into the kitchen.

"We're both ex-military, Skye. You don't have to worry that anyone is going to start shooting up the place."

"I wasn't, I mean I wouldn't, Sir. It's just that you've both had such exciting lives and it makes me feel... I don't know, naïve, I suppose."

"Your life hasn't been so easy, though, has it?"

"Lots of people have had it much worse than me, Sir." Skye ducked his head.

"Perhaps one day you'll trust me enough to be able to tell me what happened." Luke fingered a strand of Skye's silver hair. "This didn't happen for no reason."

"I was seventeen... I don't like to remember, Sir."

"And I will never push you to tell me anything you don't want to."

"Thank you, Sir. I... Soon, okay?"

Luke took Skye's hand and gave it a gentle squeeze. "When you're ready, I'll be here. A D/s relationship is not all about spankings and bondage. It's about being there for each other. A good Dominant should always listen and be prepared to guide, encourage or advise. Whatever his submissive needs."

"But it's also about what you, I mean what the Dominant needs too, isn't it?" Skye's violet eyes glistened.

"You come first. Always." Luke didn't bother to depersonalize his words. It was becoming impossible to see Skye as nothing more than a trainee sub. He had to stop deceiving himself. He wanted Skye to be his.

The moment was interrupted by Frank arriving with a pot of tea. He delivered mugs, milk and an enormous fruit cake on a plate at the same time.

"Wish I could stay and chat, but Chef is being..."

"Frank, stop gossiping and get your arse back in here!" Tor's dulcet tones sounded from the kitchen.

Frank disappeared at high speed, making Skye snicker. He fell into his natural role, pouring the tea and cutting two slices of cake, which he put on the plates Frank had left.

"This looks delicious, Sir."

"It does. Go ahead and eat." Skye had waited for his permission but soon tucked in, making the kinds of sounds that Luke would have preferred to hear in the bedroom. Amused, Luke watched him until Skye noticed and froze, a piece of cake halfway to his mouth.

"Don't stop on my account."

Skye blushed but finished his cake. As he ate his own piece, Luke had to agree that it was delicious and deserving of a pornographic soundtrack. He washed it down with a long slurp of tea.

"Could we be any more English?" Skye asked, smiling. "Tea and cake in the afternoon. We should be talking about the weather."

"Goran and I already covered that earlier," Luke said. "I think we have more important things to talk about, like how you're coping with a new job, new home and your training all at the same time. You're doing very well, you know?"

"I am?" Skye's smile lit up his face.

"Tor and Goran have both complimented your work and you fit in well with the rest of the staff. They all love you already." Skye gazed at Luke from beneath his lashes. The temptation to lean forward and kiss him was intense. "And I've been impressed with your willingness to learn. I couldn't ask for a better pupil." Skye's breath hitched. Luke suspected that tears were about to appear.

"Thank you, Sir. I want to please you so much." Skye blinked and a single wet droplet rolled down his cheek.

Luke's response was all instinct. He caught the drop of salt water with his finger, brushed it away then pressed his lips to Skye's. Skye opened for him without hesitation, the move accompanied by a gasp. Luke tasted the sweetness of his breath and any intention of restraining himself disappeared. He explored at will, memorizing how soft Skye's lips were, how warm and welcoming his mouth. Luke nipped at plump flesh and probed with his tongue, until he was forced to pull away to take a breath. Skye's eyes were glazed, his lips still parted. His breath came in rapid gasps and his arousal was apparent. Jeans that tight were not designed for concealment. He rocked on his chair, moaning, and Luke could only imagine how the plug must be torturing him. Every dominant gene in his make-up responded to the knowledge that his submissive was plugged, his cock ringed, his pleasure controlled. He wanted to strip Skye naked and reveal the harness doing its work.

"Fuck." Luke spoke in barely a whisper. His cock ached. It was only the presence of other staff in the next room that prevented him from bending Skye over the table.

"Sir?" Skye was all bewildered confusion.

"I shouldn't have done that."

"I'm glad you did. Very glad."

"You make me want things… To do things with you that wouldn't be appropriate." Skye looked utterly downcast. "That wouldn't be appropriate without a contract between us. I want you to be more than an employee, Skye. I want to train you as my submissive, not for some other man. Just thinking about anyone else laying their hands on you makes me want to lock you away." Luke clenched his fists. A gentle touch forced him to look down to where Skye was stroking his fingers, helping them relax.

"A contract, Sir?"

"Yes. One that sits alongside your contract of employment, but is separate. Something between you and me as a Dominant and submissive."

"I think I might cry again."

"That wasn't my intention." Luke laughed and took Skye's slender hand between his own. "There's no time today, but after breakfast tomorrow you and I will go somewhere quiet and talk this through properly. I'll leave a copy of the generic contract we have on file for you to read tonight. It's just a template, so don't be frightened by anything you read in it. We will tailor it to suit our needs. Together." Skye's hands were cool but his face was flushed, his eyes bright with excitement. He squirmed on his chair then moaned, squeezing his eyes shut.

"When you change for the dinner tonight, you can take the harness off," Luke said. "It won't fit under your costume and, for the moment, this sort of thing is just between you and me. It's not for sharing with an audience, however much they might enjoy it."

"Thank God!" Skye ducked his head, as if shocked at his own outburst. "Sorry, Sir, but to be honest, I'd rather be in chastity. I've been hard since you put this thing on me." Desperation broke through Skye's timidity. Luke loved that Skye felt comfortable enough to show some spirit.

"I'm sure you can deal with it for a couple more hours. Perhaps it will come in useful as a punishment in future." Luke kept a straight face as long as he could, but Skye's abject horror made him laugh.

"It's not funny, Sir!"

"No, you're right. Of course it isn't and I should be more sympathetic, but, honestly, watching you squirm, knowing the reason why, is the best entertainment a Dominant could have. Now, I think it's time that both of us got back to work, don't you?"

"Oh my God!" Skye shoved his chair back. It rocked and Luke caught it just before it fell. "What time is it? I've got so much to do, I'll never get it all finished. Everything has to be perfect."

"Calm down, sweetheart. You have plenty of time and you'll do a fantastic job if you stop panicking. You're good at this, remember? Take a few deep breaths."

Skye followed Luke's instructions and gradually calmed. "Now go. I'll come to see how you're getting on in a bit."

Skye scampered from the room then reappeared seconds later. "I should clear the table."

Luke gave him an indulgent smile. "Go. I think I can manage to clean up a couple of plates and mugs."

"Okay!" He shot back out of the door. Luke counted and got to five before Skye reappeared again.

"Kitchen. I need things from the kitchen."

Luke shook his head. He stacked crockery on the side of the table where one of the boys could pick it up later. There was no way he was setting foot in the kitchen at that moment. He headed for his office where, for once, paperwork had some appeal. He had a contract to find.

Chapter Nine

Skye stood back and cast a critical eye over the table. Everything was in its place. The place settings were evenly spaced down each side of the table, four glasses for every man. Silverware for five courses glittered in the low light alongside bone china side plates. Two ornate candelabra, loaded with dark red candles, were positioned so as not to interfere with sight lines across the table. They sat on top of a gold silk runner that was festooned with greenery. In the center sat a silver basket lined with moss, decorated to look like a nest though it lacked any hatchlings.

Nodding his satisfaction, Skye placed the name cards according to a list Tor had given him. Each card had a guest's name written in copperplate script on one side and a quote from *Brideshead Revisited* on the other.

"'O God, make me good, but not yet.'" He giggled as he read that one, which made him think of Rayne. "'To know and love one other human being is the root of all wisdom.' Now that I can agree with." He placed the card on Roy's side plate. "'I have a good mind not to take Aloysius to Venice. I don't want him to meet a lot of horrid Italian bears and pick up bad habits.' Hmm, I don't think Waugh had in mind what these guys will be thinking when they read that one."

He moved around the table adjusting the positions of knives and forks as he went. He hadn't resorted to a tape measure for the spacing because he had a good eye, but wonky spoons offended him. "'My dear, I should like to stick you full of barbed arrows like a p-p-pin cushion.' Oh wow. I hope no one takes that too literally." With the place cards done, he collected the menus, which he'd printed out on Luke's computer. They were headed with the quote, *The cream and hot butter mingled and overflowed, separating each glucose bead of caviar from its fellows, capping it in white and gold.*

"I must re-read the book," Skye murmured, slotting the menus between decorations at intervals down the table. "He writes like sex."

"Who does?"

Skye jumped, spinning in the air like a startled cat. He found Luke standing at the end of the table, wearing his glasses and looking like sin.

"Evelyn Waugh, Sir."

Luke stalked toward him. He plucked a menu from the table.

"Plovers' eggs and caviar appetizers, lobster, side of beef, Eton mess followed by a cheese course and Cointreau as an aperitif. It seems Tor has been catching up on his literature."

"The eggs are going to be served in the moss nest, Sir. Just like in the book."

"Taken from the scene where Charles first has lunch with Sebastian, as is the Cointreau. I think the other courses may be taking liberties with the text, but they're very apt. It's going to be quite a feast. And you're right—the author does have a way with words, doesn't he?"

Skye squirmed under Luke's scrutiny and, yet again, his cock hardened. He'd managed to forget the harness while he'd been absorbed in his work, but now he could think of nothing else. The plug inside him shifted like there was some kind of conspiracy going on. He bit his lower lip hard and tried to keep still. Luke looked at him over the top of his glasses, a knowing smile lightening his usual stern expression.

"You've done an amazing job. I'm going to take some pictures, but I think you should be getting upstairs to change, don't you? You only have about twenty minutes before the guests start arriving."

"I just have to put Aloysius in his place." Luke grabbed a large teddy bear from a nearby windowsill and put him in the chair at the head of the table. "There. That's everything." He gave Luke a shy smile before heading to his room, cursing the plug with every step.

In the safety of his bathroom, Skye set the shower running to heat the water then stripped off his clothes. He undid the leather belt around his waist, eased the plug from his arse then slid the ring over his cock. He dropped the entire contraption on the floor, climbed into the shower, gave his erection two hard tugs and came all over the tile with a sigh of relief.

"Oh, thank God." He pressed his forehead against the cold wall, taking a few long, slow breaths. "And now I have another confession to make." There was no time for recovery or to contemplate what his punishment might be for coming without Luke's permission. He shampooed his hair and washed with more haste than he would have liked. With a towel wrapped around his hips, he used the hairdryer to tame his unruly hair. He hadn't had a chance to check the costume that had been left in his wardrobe and at first glance he wondered if some of it was missing. Bemused, he held up the single garment and couldn't help but laugh. His 'costume' was a pair of black patent leather boxer briefs. The white front pouch had a design of three buttons and a miniature bow tie, making it look like a dress-shirt front. He didn't have time to think about it. He wriggled into the shorts, which clung to every bump and curve of his body. "Think about the positives, Skye, at least they cover everything important." There was no sign of any shoes, or instructions about wearing any, so Skye stayed barefoot and ran back downstairs. Fergus and Henry were already in the hall, wearing identical clothing to him.

"Hey, Skye, what do you think?" Fergus did a twirl. "Aren't they fabulous?"

"I, uh...if you say so."

"You're going to be the sexiest server ever. We're going to be helping Goran with the drinks. He has a whole new cocktail menu and there are going to be twizzle sticks. I don't exactly know what they are, but they sound fun."

"I wouldn't mind if Goran wanted to twizzle my stick," Henry said, grinning. "Did you see him in that harness last night? Holy hard- on, Batman!"

"Don't you two have somewhere to be?" Luke emerged from his office, a collar in his hand. "Scram." They disappeared quickly enough to be part of a magician's act. "I have a collar for you."

Skye examined the strip of leather. "It's different, Sir." He knelt at Luke's feet.

"It's a training collar. It belongs to me and you'll only take it off with my permission." Luke fastened it around Skye's neck, checking that nothing pinched. "It's a snug fit. I want you to know you're wearing it."

Skye had no doubt he would. He touched his neck, gliding his fingers along the smooth leather. Luke had positioned the buckle at the back of Skye's neck, making it less accessible, not that Skye had any intention of removing it.

"Thank you, Sir." Skye thought there was a strong chance he might cry if Luke said anything kind. "I...I mean...when I took the harness off, I..."

"Time to go to work. I'll see you last thing tonight as usual. We'll discuss your misdemeanors then." Luke brushed Skye's shoulder. It was the lightest of touches but enough to let Skye know he could stand. He took one step in the same direction Luke took before he remembered that he had an elaborate dinner party to serve. With a rueful shake of his head, he made his way to the banqueting hall, then on through to the kitchen, expecting it to be in a state of chaos. To his astonishment, a strange calm had descended and Tor, Benjy and Frank were sitting around the staffroom table, drinking tea.

"Holy cow! Look at you." Frank gaped. "That outfit is...I mean it's...practically non-existent."

"That's so fucking hot," Benjy exclaimed, eyes wide.

"I..." Skye didn't know where to put himself.

"You two. Kitchen. Now." Tor glared at his trainees. "You're embarrassing Skye."

"Sorry, Skye!"

"Yeah, sorry." The two disappeared into the kitchen.

"I apologize for their behavior," Tor said. "There's not nearly enough discipline in their lives." He gave a pained sigh. "Would you like a cup of tea before bedlam ensues?"

"No, thank you, Sir. They aren't in trouble, are they? I mean…they aren't being nasty and I am only wearing a strip of plastic." He gave his shorts a rueful glance.

Tor chuckled. "You're too sweet for your own good, Skye. No, they aren't in trouble. It's a good job you've got Luke to take care of you."

"How did you…?"

"It's obvious in every look between you and that isn't a house collar you're wearing. For what it's worth, you couldn't have found a better Dom."

Skye ducked his head, not sure what to say. Tor gave him a kind smile. "Are you ready for tonight? It's going to get frantic."

"It's about the only thing I'm sure I can do, Sir. Even if I would prefer to be fully dressed while doing it."

"Don't worry. Once they get a taste of my food, they won't be taking any notice of you."

"I'm sure that's true, Chef." Skye grinned. "I hear them coming." The sound of chatter and laughter reached them.

"The eggs should be ready. Why don't you come in and get them?"

From that moment on Skye didn't get a second's rest. He lost count of the number of trips he made between the kitchen and the banqueting hall, pushing trolley-loads of dishes. He was very glad he wasn't the one who had to deal with the washing up—industrial dishwashers had a lot going for them. On two occasions Roy and Saul sent him to fetch Tor so that everyone could congratulate him on the wonderful food. Tor was gracious and took the time to chat to everyone in a way Skye would never have had the courage to do. He served and cleared in a quiet, unobtrusive manner and managed to ensure that his presence was hardly noticed. The guests were happy to chat and relax between courses, so he had enough time to handle all ten of them by himself even if he did work up a sweat doing it. When he returned to the kitchen with the dessert dishes, Fergus and Henry were taking a break.

"We've got leftovers, Skye," Fergus said around a mouthful of beef. "This meat is amazing. So tender it melts in your mouth."

Skye slumped into a chair. Despite his skimpy clothing, he was baking hot.

"Are you okay?" asked Henry. "You're very flushed."

"Just hot and tired," Skye said. "This evening has been hard work, but worth it."

He poured himself a glass of water from a jug in the middle of the table. He gulped the cool liquid down, realizing that his throat was sore.

Fergus and Henry exchanged looks. "We'll serve the coffee and Cointreau for you, Skye. You stay here and have a rest."

Skye didn't have the energy to argue. His face was burning, but when he laid the back of his hand against his forehead, it was dry. He folded his arms and rested his head on them, resolving to close his eyes just for a few seconds. The darkness was bliss. In the quiet, he became aware of the ache behind his eyes. Then the shivering started.

"Skye?"

Skye lifted his head. His vision blurred, but he could make out Tor's shape in the doorway.

"You don't look well at all. Have you eaten anything?"

The thought of food made Skye's stomach heave. "I'm just tired. I think I was more worried about this evening than I realized."

"I suspect it's a bit more than that, Skye. Stay put. I'm going to fetch Luke." Before he left, Tor pulled a soft pullover over Skye's head. It smelled of nutmeg and cinnamon. It was far too big, but Skye was glad of its comfort and warmth. He put his head back onto the table and closed his eyes.

* * * *

"He's burning up. This isn't just tiredness," Luke said. "You were right to come and get me. You think between the two of us we can get him upstairs? He needs to be in bed, but I don't think I can carry him that far on my own. We'll have to take him via the back stairs rather than past the guests."

"He can't weigh more than a sack of flour," Tor said. "We'll have him tucked up in bed quick as you like. Just let me tell the boys what's going on. Fergus and Henry can look after the guests. Benjy and Frank just have clean-up duty. I can't imagine, after five courses, that anyone is going to be needing room service tonight, but I'll route the line through to my room just in case."

Skye didn't stir as Tor and Luke carted him down corridors and up the stairs to the staff accommodation. The only sounds he made were an occasional whimper or a rasping cough.

"I'm going to put him in my room," Luke said. "It'll be much easier for me to keep an eye on him in there."

"What if he's got something infectious?" Tor asked. "We'll be in trouble if the rest of the staff go down with whatever this as well."

"I did some medical training in the forces — just basic stuff, I'm not a doctor or anything — but I'll take his temperature and, once he's alert enough, give him paracetamol. If the fever hasn't gone down by morning, I'll call the local GP and ask her to make a house call."

"They still do that?" Tor asked.

"Yes, Tor. They do. And besides, I know Dr. Sharma well. She's a good friend."

"Okay. Well, you know where I am. If you want me to come and take a shift sitting with him while you get some rest, just give me a call. I need to let Goran know what's going on too, though I'm sure Fergus and Henry will be gossiping away down there. I wouldn't be surprised if half the county knows that Skye's ill by now."

"If any of the guests ask, just tell them he's not feeling well and leave it at that. As far as I know, nobody else is showing any signs of illness and if they do, we'll hear about it by morning."

"Is there anything else I can do, anything I can fetch for you?" Tor stood with his hands braced on his hips.

"Just take charge downstairs. Then I know I don't have to worry about anything. Do you think you can manage breakfast if Fergus and Henry help with table service?"

"Of course. I'll wait on the guests myself if I have to. Don't worry about a thing except Skye. He has to be your priority now."

Luke nodded, his attention already on the pale young man lying on his bed. "He will be. He is."

He didn't realize Tor had left until the door closed with a soft click. Luke took off his glasses and put them on the dresser, pausing briefly to finger the frames, thinking of how Skye's eyes sparkled every time he saw

Luke wearing them. Luke had never expected his less than perfect eyesight to be a turn on for a submissive, but he was quite happy that his spectacles had that effect on Skye.

He rolled up his sleeves and set to work. His first job was to remove the ridiculous shorts Skye had on. Not that he didn't look sexy wearing them, but Luke's taste ran more toward plain black leather. He rolled the PVC down Skye's thighs and off over his feet, leaving him naked apart from his collar, and Luke removed that too, cursing the position of the buckle behind Skye's neck. Next, he pulled the duvet underneath Skye's body down in slow increments so that he could lay it over him. Skye didn't stir or show any sign of waking, so Luke went to his bathroom to fetch a wet flannel. He didn't have a bowl, or anything he could put water in, so it took a few trips going to and from the bathroom sink to rinse the flannel before he was happy he'd cleaned all the dried sweat from Skye's body and the dust from his feet where he'd been barefoot.

At regular intervals, he felt Skye's forehead. His temperature spiked and descended in an irregular pattern. Sometimes his skin felt chilled and at other times burning. Luke checked for any sign of a rash, or swelling but could find no indications of a serious illness. If he had to guess, he'd say Skye was suffering from dehydration rather than any kind of infection.

There was a soft tap at the door. Luke went to open it, pressing a finger to his lips to indicate to Fergus that he should stay quiet. Fergus, his arms full of bedlinen, nodded.

"I thought you might need fresh sheets and pillow cases, Mr. Redding," he whispered. "I also have a clean duvet cover, a hot water bottle and some paracetamol in case you didn't have any up here, and a bucket full of ice. How's Skye?"

"That's very thoughtful, Fergus. Skye is sleeping. I'm sure he's going to be fine."

"Well, everybody said the same. If you need any help at all, you're to call. They all asked if there was anything more they could do and the guests send their love too. Skye has made quite an impression in the few days he's been here."

Luke swallowed, his throat dry. "I'm going to let him sleep for now, because I think he needs the rest." He stepped out into the hall, pulling the door to behind him so that he could talk to Fergus without whispering. "Have you noticed how much Skye has been eating and drinking? Do you think you could ask the others? I suspect he's dehydrated. I imagine he's been so busy he hasn't thought about needing to drink regularly."

"He's always eaten at the meals I've shared with him, though he doesn't take very big portions," Fergus said. "But I'm not sure about the evenings. Most of us have time to take a break and grab something from the kitchen, but he's so busy at that time of day he may not have. Henry and I keep bottles of water with us, and I know Tor makes Benjy and Frank drink all the time in the heat of the kitchen, but I haven't noticed Skye drinking very much, so you could be right. I'll ask the others, though."

"Thanks. Could you ask Tor if he could spare a bowl of some kind that I can fill with water? It's a pain to have to keep running backward and forward to the bathroom. Oh, and perhaps he or one of the boys could make some soup in the morning. I doubt Skye will feel like eating very much, but he'll need nutrition."

"Of course, Mr. Redding." Fergus handed over the supplies then scampered down the corridor to carry out his mission.

Luke went back into his bedroom, putting everything onto a chair. Skye had changed position on the bed, curling into a ball beneath the duvet. He made quiet, whimpering noises as if he were having a bad dream.

Luke sat on the edge of the bed and stroked Skye's silver hair away from his forehead. "Hush, sweetheart. I'm right here and you're going to be fine. I think you'd be surprised to know how many people here at The Retreat want to take care of you. You're an easy man to love."

Skye's lashes fluttered and he opened his eyes. "Luke? What happened?"

"Welcome back," Luke said, helping Skye to sit up against his pillows. "You're sick. Tor and I carried you up here. You're in my bed."

"I don't remember... Oh, my head hurts. And I'm thirsty, my throat is a bit sore. Do I have the flu or something?"

"I'm not sure yet, but don't worry, you'll feel better soon."

"What about the guests?" A panicked expression fixed itself on Skye's face and he made to get out of bed. "I need to get downstairs... Oh, I'm naked."

Luke maneuvered Skye's legs back beneath the covers. "If you try to get out of this bed again without my permission, I will spank you so hard you won't be able to sit for a week. The guests are fine. Everything is under control. You have one thing to do, one thing to think about, and that's getting better."

Luke wasn't sure if the pink flush on Skye's cheek bones was due to his fever, or the mention of a spanking. He hid a smile. "Do you feel up to taking a shower? I gave you a wipe down with a flannel, but standing in cool water will help to bring your temperature down. You need to take some paracetamol too."

"A shower sounds really good."

"Okay. You stay there while I get everything ready." Luke grabbed the internal phone and called Tor. "He's awake, Tor. Can you let everyone know? And it would be great if one of the boys could come and change the bed while he has a shower. Fergus brought me clean sheets earlier. They're in my bedroom." He listened for a few seconds then clicked the phone off. It didn't take him long to set the shower running and to make sure there were towels on the heated rail. He helped Skye out of bed and kept an arm around his waist as he walked on wobbly legs into the bathroom.

"Did you undress me, Sir?" Skye's fingers strayed to his neck as if searching for the collar."

"I did. It didn't take long—there wasn't much to take off. Your collar is on the dresser and it will be back around your neck just as soon as you're well. Collars and sore throats aren't a sensible combination." Luke looked at his double-width shower. "Are you going to be able to manage in there on your own?"

Skye gave him a weak smile. "I think so, Sir." He got beneath the spray, leaning on the wall for balance.

"I'm not so sure." Luke stripped off his clothes then stepped into the shower behind Skye. "All you have to do is stand there. Rest your hands on the tiles if it helps you balance. If you feel faint, or unwell, tell me straight away."

Skye's eyes were glassy, his face even more flushed than before. He stood, passive, as Luke smoothed shower gel over his body and lathered the shampoo into his hair.

"It feels good, Sir. Thank you."

"It's my pleasure." Luke tried to remain detached, but running his hands all over Skye's slender body had an inevitable effect, plumping his cock into hardness. He ignored it and concentrated on rinsing shampoo from Skye's hair. Skye's eyes were drifting shut, and he wobbled.

"I think that's enough. We're done. Let's get out of here before you fall over." Luke wrapped a towel around his hips then positioned Skye so that his feet were on the warm mat rather than cold tile. Docile and dreamy, Skye stood still while Luke wrapped him in a bath towel. He used a second, smaller towel to rub most of the water from Skye's hair before patting his body dry.

"You'll do. Let's get you back into bed."

Skye nodded. He made it to the bed, but it was a close thing and he fell rather than climbed in. The sheets and duvet cover had been changed and Luke was grateful that whichever one of the boys had been into the room had been quiet and discreet. He'd have to think of a suitable reward for his staff once Skye was better.

"You can sleep soon, sweetheart, but I want you to take a couple of tablets first."

Skye took the two pills that Luke handed him, swallowing them with water from a glass that he drained to the bottom.

"I'm so tired."

"You can sleep now, for as long as you need. The others will cover your duties tomorrow and for however long they need to."

"I'm sorry..."

"You have nothing to apologize for. Just rest, I'll be right here." Luke pulled up the covers. "I'm going to put some pyjamas on and sleep in the chair, just over there."

Skye reached for him, "Don't leave me, Sir. Please. Could you, I mean would you mind, sleeping in the bed with me?"

Luke considered the situation for a few seconds but, as it was clear that Skye would be distressed if Luke didn't comply with his wishes, it wasn't a difficult decision to make.

"If that's what you want." He squeezed Skye's hand. Skye smiled and the lines of tension on his forehead smoothed. His eyes drifted shut and by the time Luke had dug a pair of rarely used pajama bottoms from a drawer, Skye was sound asleep.

Chapter Ten

Luke didn't get a lot of sleep. Sometime during the night, Skye had turned into an octopus, his arms and legs spread across Luke's body. The close contact was torment, but Luke didn't have the heart to move Skye as he nuzzled beneath Luke's chin, loose strands of hair tickling his nose. Skye talked in his sleep, though the words didn't make much sense. The only one that Luke could make out was 'dad', which Skye repeated several times.

His fever returned and Skye threw the covers back, exposing them both to the cool night air. Half an hour later, he started shivering. Luke retrieved the covers and held him close until he calmed. Luke saw three a.m. pass on his digital clock then managed a light doze until just after six when Skye awoke with a start. It took him a while to realize where he was.

"Oh my God, I'm so sorry, Sir." He rolled away from Luke's body. "What am I doing in your bed?"

"You don't remember?"

"Did I drink alcohol last night?" Skye asked. "My head is pounding."

Luke pulled himself up and sat back against the headboard. "You got sick. You had a fever. Do you not remember anything?"

"Did we have a shower? Together? That must have been a dream."

"We did. You were a bit shaky to say the least. Apart from a headache, how are you feeling?" Luke laid the back of his hand against Skye's forehead, which was still warmer than it should be.

"I ache a bit, but, apart from that, not too bad."

Luke swung his legs over the side of the bed then stood. He stretched and every joint in his body seem to pop. "I'm going to go downstairs and fetch some fruit juice. I'll see if I can find the thermometer from the first aid kit too. I want to take your temperature now you're alert enough not to bite off the end of the thing." He grabbed his robe from the back of the door but just as he was about to open it, someone knocked. Luke grinned as Skye took a dive beneath the covers so that only the top of his head was showing. "There's no point in hiding, Skye. They all know you're in here." He walked through to the lounge then opened the door to find Rayne standing in the corridor.

"Tor sent me up here to see if there's anything you need, Mr. Redding." Rayne bounced on his toes. He had far too much energy for the time of day, in Luke's humble opinion.

"Actually, Rayne, you can make yourself useful. I was just about to go downstairs to get some juice, so if you could fetch that for me it would be a real help. Find the first aid kit that Tor keeps in the kitchen and bring me the thermometer from it. Some fruit and toast would be great if there's anyone available in the kitchen.

"Everyone's up already. We were all worried about Skye. Is he okay?" Rayne tried to peek around the doorway. "Hey, Skye. Hope you're feeling better. Everyone sends you their love. You know I can see your hair, right?"

A groan came from beneath the duvet.

"Rayne, go fetch the juice."

"Sure, right, yes. I won't be long, promise."

Luke closed the door with a sigh. He returned to the bedroom. "I think you're going to be getting a lot of visitors today."

"I should be working, I need to lay for breakfast…"

"If you mention working once more, I'm going to chain you to the bed. I'd rather reserve that for when you're feeling better, but needs must."

Skye peeked from beneath the duvet. "Sorry, Sir."

"I want you to drink another glass of water, and swallow some more paracetamol. When Rayne gets back I'll take your temperature and if it's too high I'm going to call out the doctor."

"I don't feel that bad, Sir. I wouldn't want to waste a doctor's time."

"Your health is not a waste of time for anyone, Skye, so stop arguing and do as you're told."

"Yes, Sir." Skye took the medication and drank a glass of water. "What do you think is wrong with me? I don't get sick very often, just the odd cold every now and again, the same as anyone else. I had chickenpox as a kid, I think. That's the itchy one, right?"

"It is. My guess is that you haven't been eating and drinking enough over the last few days and that you got dehydrated. That, combined with the stress of a new job, built up and your body decided it was time to rest. You have to look after yourself better and I'll be making sure you do. I haven't been doing a very good job of taking care of you, have I?"

"It's not your fault, Sir." Skye nibbled on his lower lip. "I haven't had much appetite."

"A day or two in bed, gallons of water and some of Tor's home cooking and you'll be right as rain, I'm sure. Are you warm enough?" Skye's bare chest was distracting.

"One minute I'm boiling hot and the next I'm freezing cold."

Luke dug around in his dresser drawer and pulled out a long-sleeved T-shirt. It was old, but soft. "Here, put this on. You can always take it off again if you get too hot."

Skye pulled the garment over his head. It was too big and the sleeves were too long, so he rolled them up. "Thanks, it's perfect. Um... Sir? I need to go to the bathroom."

"Go ahead but leave the door open in case you feel faint or need help."

"I'm kind of naked from the waist down." Skye peeked beneath the covers as if he needed confirmation.

"It's such a shame that I only have one pair of pyjamas, and I'm wearing them," Luke said, grinning. "But there has to be some compensation for being your mattress all night."

There was a distinct sway to Skye's hips as he made his way to the bathroom.

"Cheeky little brat," Luke murmured. "He's feeling better."

Skye did as he'd been asked and left the bathroom door ajar while he used the toilet and swilled his face. He emerged with bright eyes and rosy cheeks, pulling on the hem of his top in a vain attempt to cover his groin. He avoided making eye contact and scuttled into bed, yanking the covers up to his chest.

"It's nothing I haven't seen before, Skye," Luke said with a wry smile. "And will be seeing a lot of in the future." There was a light tap at the outer door. "Saved by the... Knock." Luke opened the door to find Tor standing in the corridor, hefting a sizeable tray. "Here." He held the door open. "Come through to the bedroom. Let me clear a space on the dresser for that." He moved a few bits and pieces aside so that there was room for Tor to put the tray down.

"You're looking a bit better this morning, Skye. You were as white as a sheet yesterday evening, but now you've got some color. You no doubt need some of my food inside you." Tor removed the covers from the plates on the tray. "I brought plain toast, but there's homemade marmalade if you want to cheer it up a bit. Then there's a plate of sliced melon and some strawberries. Fresh fruit juice, or milk to drink. I didn't think coffee was a very good idea, in case you need to sleep more, so there's just an individual cafetière for you, Luke. Rayne also dug out the thermometer from the first aid kit and it's on the side of the tray."

"That's perfect. Thanks, Tor." Luke picked up the thermometer, removed the cover then gave it a shake. "Once Skye has eaten and is settled, I'll be down, Tor, though I'm sure you and the boys have everything under control. I'll probably bring some work up here later on so that I can keep an eye on the patient." He approached the side of the bed. "Open wide." He slipped the thermometer beneath Skye's tongue. "And close. We'll leave that in there for a minute or so. If you could hang on until I get the reading, Tor. If it's too high, I'll get you to call the doctor."

"Sure. I'll ask one of the boys to bring up a few more bottles of water and some fresh ice. You need to stay hydrated, Skye."

Luke withdrew the thermometer from Skye's mouth and squinted at the reading. Without his glasses it was difficult to see. "Dead on a hundred. That's manageable. I'll take it again in a few hours just to make sure."

"A low-grade fever," Tor said. "I think you're right about the dehydration, Luke. If he doesn't develop any more symptoms today, it's unlikely to be the flu."

"Agreed."

Tor made for the door. "Make sure you look after yourself, Skye, and do as you're told. Let me know when he's ready for visitors, Luke. All the boys will want to come up here and check on him."

"Tell them they have to wait until this afternoon," Luke said. "I want him to get some more sleep before the hordes descend."

"I'll have that water put outside the door."

Luke was glad to be left alone with Skye and relieved that his condition didn't seem to be serious. "Do you think you can eat something?" he asked.

"I'm not very hungry, Sir, but I'll try."

"Breakfast in bed should work." Luke picked up the tray. He settled next to Skye, resting the tray on his lap. "Have some juice first."

Skye took the glass. He took a small sip, then a longer drink. "So good…" He drained the rest in one go. "I don't know why I'm so thirsty."

"It's your body telling you to drink more and if you won't obey it, you'll obey me. Toast or fruit?"

"Fruit please, Sir."

Luke speared a cube of melon then held it to Skye's lips. The flush on Skye's cheeks deepened, but he opened his mouth and accepted Luke's offering.

"So sweet and juicy."

Luke was grateful for the length of his robe, because feeding Skye pieces of fruit was an intense erotic experience. Skye made no attempt to take control but waited for each new mouthful to be raised for him to take. He relaxed against his pillows, making the sweetest sounds as he enjoyed the succulent fruits.

"Enough?" Luke gauged that Skye was chewing slower.

"Yes, thank you, Sir." Skye tried to hide a yawn. "I could drink the milk though." He glugged it down, then yawned again.

"Don't try to stay awake. More sleep won't do you any harm at all."

"Are you going to stay with me, Sir?"

"If I leave, it will only be to go downstairs for a few minutes, then I'll be back. No getting out of bed if I'm not here, okay?"

"'kay." Skye slipped beneath the covers. He turned onto his side and his eyes drifted shut. Soon, his breathing slowed. Luke ate some toast and drank his coffee before sliding off the bed. Skye mumbled and his brow furrowed as if he were concerned about Luke's absence.

"I'm still here, Skye." Luke kept his voice low, hoping that subliminal reassurance would be enough. It seemed to work because Skye snuffled then settled and his breathing evened out. Luke envied him and for a few seconds contemplated joining him, but he couldn't. His conscience wouldn't allow him to abandon his job when The Retreat was full of guests deserving of his intention.

Craving more coffee, he dressed in his usual working attire of plain black trousers and pale blue dress shirt. He pulled on socks and laced his shoes, keeping an eye on Skye in case the rustling disturbed him. In sleep, Skye was even more beautiful. He half-smiled as if dreaming about something enjoyable. Luke was loath to leave him but resolved to be as quick as possible. Though he trusted Tor to have everything under control, he had to run a busy kitchen and couldn't be all over the minute details that made The Retreat such a special place for its guests.

Taking the tray, Luke made his way downstairs. The big table in the banqueting hall was already laid for breakfast—Fergus and Henry both scurrying around making last-minute adjustments and bickering over who was doing a better job until they spotted Luke.

"Good morning, Mr. Redding," they chorused.

"Good morning, boys. It looks like you are doing a good job there."

"Not as good as Skye does," Fergus piped up. "Tor said he's feeling better. Will he be coming down today?"

"Not today," Luke said. "He's confined to bed."

Henry giggled. "Sounds fun."

"You two brats are incorrigible." Luke sighed and made his way through to the kitchen where he found Tor and his crew hard at work. Luke left his tray on a clear area of counter.

"Any chance of some more coffee?" he asked as soon as he caught Tor's eye.

"I guess you didn't get a whole lot of sleep last night," Tor said. He sent Benjy toward the coffeemaker with a flick of his finger.

"Not much. It's been quite a while since I had to deal with sleep deprivation. I'm out of practice. I don't want to leave Skye alone too long because his temperature is still a bit up and down. He's sleeping at the moment, so I'm going to grab some paperwork from the office and head back upstairs."

"What do you think he could handle for lunch?"

"He just had fruit and juice for breakfast, so something light. Soup perhaps? I know it's a bit of a cliché."

"Yes, after you mentioned it last night, I dug out some fantastic soup recipes that I haven't had a chance to try and there should be plenty of home-made bread left over from breakfast. Do you want me to bring a tray up?"

Luke shook his head. "No, I'll come down and fetch it around twelve-thirty if that's okay? It'll give me a chance to collect some more work and I'll need to stretch my legs a bit."

"Well, the plans for today are straightforward. Rayne is taking out a group of four who are heading for some retail therapy and sightseeing in Oxford, so they'll be gone most of the day. One of the subs went to university there and wants to show his Dom his old haunts apparently. The rest of the group are staying here and haven't put in any special requests."

"And tonight's angels and devils theme?"

"Fergus and Henry have their costumes—red leather thongs and horns." Tor grinned.

"Appropriate. Those two are demons in disguise." Secretly, Luke was glad that Skye would avoid parading around almost naked.

"Goran told me last night that he has a halo, which I'm having difficulty imagining. He said he wouldn't be down for breakfast, which isn't a surprise because it was a very late night last night and he did all the clearing up before he went to bed. He said he'd be around for lunchtime drinks if any of the guests want anything other than Alka-Seltzer. Roy and Saul have requested a light lunch, just sandwiches and salad, which they can come and help themselves to when they're ready, so there won't be much service needed. Tonight's menu is agreed and the boys will be helping set everything up in the dungeon, because that's where we're serving the meal this evening."

"Those red light bulbs I ordered are in a box under my desk in the office. Just send one of the boys to get them later. They should know where the rest of the decorations are stored. If you think you'll need him, then enlist Rayne's help tonight. He can wear Skye's costume. They aren't that much different in size."

"Another one well suited to horns."

"Your coffee is ready, Mr. Redding." Benjy ambled over. "I have a clean mug for you and I've made up the coffee how you like it and put it into a flask so it will stay hot. There should be enough to tide you over until lunchtime."

"That's very thoughtful, Benjy. Thank you."

Benjy beamed then headed back to his station.

"Right, I'll leave you to it. You know where I am if you need me." Clutching his flask and mug, Luke made a quick stop in his office for his laptop before making his way back upstairs. Skye was still fast asleep and hadn't even changed position so Luke settled at the desk that sat beneath his window. He could keep an eye on Skye through the open bedroom door. As Luke waited for his laptop to come to life, he stared at the treeline. A layer of mist hovered above the ground, blurring the lines of trunks and branches. A bird of prey hovered, seeking breakfast. The speed of its dive was breathtaking, but it wheeled away, talons empty, crying its frustration into the wind. Luke felt a momentary pang of sympathy for its failure, counterpointed by relief for whatever small creature had escaped. If only his own life could be so simple. He stared at his screen, not seeing the accounts he'd opened. He swiveled on his chair to stare at the young man in his bed.

Skye's lips were parted, his cheeks still flushed, but his breathing was slow and even. The covers had slipped enough to expose a shoulder, giving Luke cause to regret lending Skye his top. Skye had the kind of flawless skin that deserved to be on view.

"But only my view," Luke murmured. He turned back to his laptop, resolving to focus on his work so that he could give Skye his full attention once he awoke.

He got much more done that he'd thought he would because Skye slept for four more hours. Luke tested the temperature of his forehead twice and by lunchtime it seemed to be returning to normal and some of the colour in his cheeks had faded. He stirred then woke with a sigh and a smile.

"I was having the most amazing dream," he said.

"Sounds intriguing," Luke replied, making his way to the side of the bed.

"Luke! Sir…I mean, I forgot where I was."

"We can discuss your dream later if you remember it. How are you feeling?"

"Better! My headache is gone and I'm warm but not hot and icky."

Luke grabbed the thermometer anyway. "Let me check." After a short wait he extracted the instrument from Skye's mouth. "Normal. Excellent."

"That's great! So I can get up and go back to work."

"You will do no such thing. You'll spend the day resting."

"But I…"

Luke went to the wardrobe and retrieved a tie from its hanger. Plain dark blue silk, it would do very well for what he had in mind. He looped one end around Skye's left wrist, making sure he knotted it in such a way that Skye wouldn't be able to slip his hand free. The other end, he fastened to the headboard. Skye gaped, his eyes wide.

"I warned you earlier today what would happen if you talked about going back to work again. The tie is a compromise, because, believe me, if I had a pair of handcuffs up here, you'd be in them."

Skye gave his wrist an experimental tug. He could free himself using his other hand, but he settled, as if accepting the bondage as Luke's right. "You always keep your word, don't you, Sir?"

"Always." Luke tried to keep his expression stern, but failed. Skye looked so sweet and innocent, yet the bed clothes were tented and Luke had a vivid picture of Skye's nudity beneath the covers in his head. "I'm going downstairs to fetch some lunch. You will stay put until I get back and if you behave, I'll let the boys come up to visit this afternoon. They can take it in turns to keep you company while I work."

Skye slipped his free hand beneath the covers.

"And no touching, in case you were in any doubt." By the time he made it out to the corridor, Luke was grinning.

Chapter Eleven

Watching his friends dance to *Devil Woman* wearing red leather thongs and horns had Skye laughing so hard he had a coughing fit. Rayne pressed a fresh bottle of water into his free hand.

"I can't believe Luke tied you to his bed. Well, actually I can, because he's Luke and that's just the kind of thing he'd do, and it's hot...but it means you can't dance with us, which is so not fair. How often do I get to strut my stuff around here? You'll just have to pretend to be sick for a bit longer."

"I'm not going to do that, Rayne. I want to get back to work. I don't like that you and the others have to pick up my slack." Skye pouted.

"That's because you are sweet and nice. What do you two think you're doing?" Benjy and Frank were play wrestling on the floor at the end of the bed, limbs tangled, both in hysterics. "They need mud, or foam... Or jelly! That would be even better. Can you picture it, Skye? A pit of strawberry jelly and lots of slippery skin-on-skin contact. Yum!"

Skye almost spat his mouthful of water across the bed. Instead, he choked and started coughing again. The door opened and Luke, glasses perched on the end of his nose and carrying several folders, stepped into the room. Benjy and Frank scrambled to their feet while Rayne inched toward the door

"Time we were all going," Rayne said. "Glad you're feeling better, Skye. We miss you." He gave Luke a sheepish grin.

How Luke managed to keep a straight face while the three semi-naked young men scrambled out of the door, Skye had no idea. He lay still and tried to look innocent.

"I leave you alone for one hour and come back to find some kind of orgy going on in here. Exactly what have the four of you been up to? I'm sure those boys were fully dressed when they arrived."

"They wanted to show me their costumes for the angels and devils party tonight. Rayne had his iPod and mini speakers and said that the only way to show the outfits off properly was to dance. He put together a playlist where all the songs either had devil or angel in the title. It all went downhill from there, Sir." Skye displayed his bound wrist. "But I didn't get out of bed, Sir. Promise."

"You're flushed again." Luke placed his folders on the desk then grabbed the thermometer. "Open."

Skye sat with the thermometer sticking out of his mouth for a full minute and tried to think thoughts other than how gorgeous Luke looked in his glasses. When Luke extracted the instrument from his mouth, Skye kept his fingers crossed that his temperature would still be normal.

"It's fine," Luke said. "Those boys just got you overexcited, didn't they? No more visitors for you today."

Skye attempted to look suitably remorseful. Luke massaged the bridge of his nose, frowning. "I brought up a copy of the generic contract for us to look through together, but perhaps it should wait until tomorrow."

"No! I mean... I'm fine, Sir." Skye detected a twinkle in Luke's eyes. "You're teasing me!"

"Perhaps." Luke undid the tie around Skye's wrist. "Would you like to take a shower after being in bed all day?"

"Yes, please, Sir. That would be wonderful."

"If you're still feeling fine once you're done, you can get dressed. We'll look through the paperwork together. While you're in the bathroom, I'll call Tor and ask him to send up something light for supper. It will have to be sandwiches, or salad because they're very busy in the kitchen with the final preparations for tonight's dinner."

"I'm not very hungry, Sir. I'm still full from the soup we had at lunchtime."

"You still need to eat something," Luke said, his tone stern. "Or I'll take some convincing that you're fit enough to go back to work tomorrow."

As he swung his legs out of bed, Skye resolved to eat everything he was offered. He couldn't face another day in bed, doing nothing. He stripped off his borrowed top before walking naked into the bathroom, pleased that his show wasn't lost on Luke who muttered something under his breath about brats in need of spankings.

Skye took his time in the bathroom, partly because he wanted to think through what was about to happen and partly because he wanted to look his best for the man who was going to become his Dominant. It was like winning the lottery. Skye couldn't believe how lucky he was. He'd thought himself fortunate to be under Luke's tutelage in the first place, but for Luke to propose a personal contract between them was more than he could ever have hoped for. His feelings for Luke grew by the hour and Skye suspected he might be in love—not that he knew how that was supposed to feel. If it was about the rush of joy he felt every time Luke walked into a room, or the concern that welled up when Luke seemed tired, or just the physical reaction of his body when Luke looked at him as if he mattered...then it was love. He didn't care that it had happened so fast. He trusted his instincts.

Once he was finished, Skye hung the wet towel on the rack. He had nothing to wear so went back into the bedroom as he was. Luke was at the desk in the lounge, working, but turned around to give him an appreciative stare.

"Much as I'd like to keep you naked," he said, "it wouldn't be appropriate while we're discussing the contract. I'm not making any promises for later, though. I went to your room while you were in the shower and fetched some clothes for you. They're on the bed."

Images of what might happen later on that night filled Skye's head. He distracted himself by pulling on the jeans Luke had selected, then the soft pale blue pullover that was one of his favorites. Luke hadn't provided underwear, and the rub of denim against Skye's cock did nothing for his self-control. He suspected that it was a deliberate move on Luke's part.

He doubted the man did anything without thinking through the consequences first.

"Come and sit down," Luke said. He took one of the armchairs near the fire. Skye took the other one, perching on the edge of the seat. He was far too nervous and excited to relax. He touched his neck, wishing that Luke's collar was still in place. In contrast, Luke seemed at ease, the papers in his hand held steady.

"You should know, I haven't done this before," Luke said. "I've witnessed contracts for other people and been involved in paperwork for all the staff here, but I've never had my own submissive." He pushed his glasses up his nose.

"Then this is a first for both of us, Sir. I'm glad." Skye was shocked at his own bravery. Luke gave him courage.

"It's important that you feel able to speak your mind. If there's anything that bothers you, tell me. This agreement keeps you safe."

Skye didn't think a piece of paper could make him feel any safer than he already did with Luke, but he understood that a formal agreement made sense.

"There are all kinds of contracts and no one right way of doing this," Luke said, settling back in his chair. "Some can be really detailed, but the one I have here is quite simple. It can grow with us. Its main purpose is to define the standards expected of you as a submissive and me, as your Dominant. It's also an important, symbolic representation of the commitment between us."

Luke's use of the word *commitment* sent a thrill of pleasure through Skye's body.

"When you sign this, if you sign it, you must be giving your informed consent."

"Yes, Sir. I know what I'm doing."

"You and I both have expectations and desires. It's important we articulate them and that the contract meets both our needs." Luke handed Skye two sheets of paper, stapled together. "Take a look. I'll give you time to read it again later. There are a few things we need to agree and the first is the period of our arrangement. I suggest six months initially, with an option to extend at any time."

"I think that's about right, Sir. It's long enough for a fair trial, for us to get to know each other properly."

"Good." Luke smiled. "There's a section on our roles and duties, and another about punishment. That's me punishing you, in case you were wondering."

Skye snickered. "I kind of worked that one out, Sir. But punishment isn't the same as discipline, is it?"

"No. I'll administer discipline every evening. Punishment is to correct disobedience or dishonesty. I'll always explain why I think a punishment is necessary and I'll tell you what it will be. It will always be defined and never open-ended. Your safe word still applies and that's what the next area of the contract covers. There's an important bit about the limitations to my authority and respect for your safe word."

"What do you mean by limitations, Sir?"

"This isn't a contract between Master and slave. You're an independent person agreeing to submit to my authority and guidance. That doesn't mean you abdicate responsibility for your own well-being. I expect your honesty at all times. If you're worried or anxious about anything at all, you speak to me. Your safe word is sacrosanct at all times, without exception. Use it and everything stops, but then we talk about why you've used it, okay? I can't make things better if I don't know what the problems are. I'm not perfect and I'm going to make mistakes."

"You make it sound like I have all the power here," Skye said, intrigued.

"That's because you do. Only you can grant me control over your body. That's not something I can take from you and I wouldn't want to. We must both be willing participants in this, aware of what we both need. I need to be in control, to be in charge, and you…"

"I want someone to take me out of myself, to help me make decisions. I want to take care of you too. That's okay, isn't it? I need to feel useful, that I'm making a contribution and not just taking from you all the time." Skye pulled his knees up and hugged them.

"It's more than okay. Then finally, there's a bit about terminating the relationship and why it can be ended. We both sign it, then I'll ask Tor to witness it for me and you can ask a friend to witness it for you too. The witnesses can ask you questions to make sure the contract is what you want, that you don't feel any sense of obligation. If you change your mind, or want to wait a while, that's fine and it will have no effect on your job here. How does that all sound? Is there anything you want to ask?"

"Well, I was kind of expecting a tick list of things I would and wouldn't do. I mean…there are things I'd like to try, but other things scare me."

"There are contracts like that, but I'd prefer that we discuss those things when they arise. I already know you enjoy bondage and chastity. If I want to introduce anything new into a scene, I'll discuss it with you first."

"That sounds good, Sir. I don't think I have any other questions."

"Then I want you to take the paperwork to your room and read it through again on your own. If you decide you have more questions, that's fine."

Skye had no doubt that he would sign the contract. The words he and Luke had agreed on together made everything fall into place. He was amazed at how a fragile piece of paper could represent the solid foundations of their burgeoning relationship. If it had been etched onto a stone tablet, Skye wouldn't have seen it as any more permanent. Luke's wishes were paramount, however, so Skye took the document back to his room to read alone. He had never been so certain of anything in his life. He couldn't wait to scrawl his signature in the space provided then get on with being Luke's submissive.

Trainee submissive. He had to keep it in his head that he still needed a lot of training to become the man Luke wanted him to be—that he wanted to be. A little ink wasn't going to result in fireworks or some kind of earth-shattering change, but it did mean that Luke wanted him.

Me. He wants me. Not some other, perfect sub. He doesn't mind that I'm clumsy sometimes, that loud noises and crowds scare me, that I only have vague notions of what I want to do with my life. He read the pages four times, until the words were etched into his brain. He didn't want Luke to think that he hadn't taken his direction seriously. He fidgeted, lying on the bed, then paced his room before deciding to go and find Rayne. He made sure to put a fleece jacket on over his sweater and thick socks and boots on his feet. He guessed Luke's definition of looking after himself included warm clothes. It probably didn't include an outing to the garages so soon after being ill, but that was where he was most likely to find Rayne, even in the early evening.

He made it to the entrance hall without being seen, but then Goran appeared from the snug, a crate of glasses in his arms.

"Skye! Does Luke know you're down here?"

Skye stared at the floor. "No, Goran. I mean, he knows I'm out of bed and everything. I need to find Rayne."

"Why don't you go and wait in the snug? I'll track the brat down for you."

"Oh, I don't want to be any trouble. I can—"

"You can go—"

"Wait in the snug. Yes, Goran." Skye knew it wasn't a battle worth fighting. Goran chuckled and headed toward a storage cupboard with his box.

The snug was one of Skye's favorite rooms at The Retreat. It was how he imagined he'd like his home to be one day—cozy, warm and welcoming. He loved to browse the bookshelves, picking at random because he liked the color of a spine or because the title sparked his interest. He wished he had more time to read, especially history books, which had always been his first love. He picked a volume on the English Civil War then settled in an armchair beneath the warm glow of a standard lamp, his precious papers tucked next to his thigh. His head was deep into the Battle of Edgehill in 1642 when Rayne arrived.

"Brains and beauty. You have a ridiculous advantage over the rest of us, you know." Rayne threw himself into the chair next to Skye. "Goran dragged me out of the garage and told me to come find you in here. That man is fine."

"I didn't take you away from anything important, did I?"

"Actually I was hiding in the car listening to a podcast of last week's episodes of *The Archers* on my iPod." Rayne giggled. "I only had another five minutes to go. I would have had to come in soon anyway because I'm helping out at tonight's dinner and a little bit of manscaping is required if I have to display my hot bod in that teensy costume."

"I'm sorry you have to do my job as well as your own. I tried to tell Luke that I'd be okay to work tonight but he—"

"Got all protective and insisted you weren't well enough yet?"

Sky nodded. "I'm afraid so. Though I have to confess I'm quite glad I don't have to dress up tonight. That costume is minuscule."

"It is, isn't it? I'm intending to make as many trips back to the kitchen as possible while I'm wearing it. I want to make sure Tor gets an eyeful of my hotness."

"He'll spank you again."

"Oh God, I hope so." Rayne shifted in his seat. "Gets me all horny just thinking about it. But we're not here to talk about me. Goran said you needed me for something, so what can I do to help?"

Skye closed his book then placed it on the floor by his feet. He handed the contract to Rayne. "Luke and I, well... We..."

"Oh my God, is this a contract?" Rayne bounced to his feet then did an excited circuit of the room, waving the papers.

"Yes. Can you sit down, Rayne? You're making me feel giddy." Skye rolled his eyes. "Luke insists I have a friend read it and witness my signature. Apparently, it's something to do with making sure that I'm not under any duress or pressure, especially because Luke is my boss."

"And you're asking me?" Skye nodded. "That makes me your best friend in the whole wide world, doesn't it?" Rayne retook his seat, sitting cross-legged. "I'm honored that you've asked me, I really am." He read for a while then looked up. "You agreed all this together, right?"

"Of course. Earlier this evening. We sat down and Luke took me through it line by line. I would have been quite happy to sign it there and then."

"And you're sure this is what you want?"

"I've never been surer of anything in my life. I trust him, Rayne. I'm not exactly experienced and he's so patient, so in control of everything."

"I'm not surprised. Luke Redding is hot as hell and he'd walk over hot coals for any of us. Have you and he...?"

Skye's face heated. "Rayne! That's none of your business."

"But now we're officially besties, you're obliged to tell me everything. It's an unwritten rule." He tapped his fingers on one knee. "Waiting."

"Have you and Tor?" Skye figured his best form of defense was a question.

"I wish! I've never even seen him with his shirt off, and that in itself is a tragedy. It's not like I haven't offered myself up on a platter, well-seasoned and prepped if you get my meaning. The man must be celibate—though that would be a heinous waste of a good Dom."

"Heinous?"

"Heard it on some documentary about mass murderers." Rayne handed Skye the contract. "Of course I'll sign it. Do you want me to do it now or is there a formal thing going on?"

"Oh, I don't know. Luke didn't say. I suppose he might want you to sign it at the same time as Tor. I'll have to let you know."

"I need to get going," Rayne said, scrambling from the chair. "Angels and devils wait for no man — and my sweetmeats will be in Tor's stew pot if I'm late."

"God forbid. I should get back too. I imagine Luke thinks I'm snuggled up in bed, not down here with you."

"If he catches you, then my balls won't be the only ones in danger."

"Thanks, Rayne. For being here, I mean."

"Anytime, gorgeous. Now go back to bed or Luke won't be using his tie to keep you there. It'll be something metal with a big padlock."

"On the odd occasion, Rayne, you actually say something intelligent."

"Sir!" Skye and Rayne spoke at the same time. Luke stood in the doorway, holding two steaming mugs.

"Sorry, Skye. Friendship only goes so far, even if you are my bestie. You're on your own." Rayne scuttled toward the door, edging past Luke with a sheepish grin.

Skye didn't know whether to stay put or get to his knees. He met Luke's steady gaze.

"How are you feeling?"

"Good, thank you, Sir. A little tired."

"I brought some hot chocolate."

"How did you know I was here, Sir?"

"Goran came to find me. He told me he had to stop you from going outside in the cold." Luke came over and sat in Rayne's recently vacated chair. "You don't need my permission to leave your room, Skye, but I would prefer you didn't venture into the grounds when it's sub-zero and dark. Not until I'm happy you're recovered at least."

"I'm sorry, Sir. I was so excited about the contract and I couldn't wait to tell Rayne all about it." Skye hated the thought that he'd done something to upset Luke. "He says he'll be my witness, but I wasn't sure if he should go ahead and sign or if you wanted him to do it at the same time as Tor."

"That's good news. It would be nice for them to do it together, don't you think?" There was a hint of mischief in Luke's eyes, which made Skye snicker.

"I think you're a very naughty Dom, Sir. Oh...I didn't mean to say that out loud!"

"I can't imagine why you should think that." Luke kept a straight face. "Have some hot chocolate." He handed over the mug and Skye welcomed the distraction, breathing in the sweet scent.

"Oh, wow, marshmallows!" He poked at the pink blobs floating on the surface of the deep brown liquid.

"Frank made it and he insisted they were a requirement. I drew the line at whipped cream."

"I can think of a few other things to do with that," Skye whispered. He peeked at Luke from beneath his lashes.

"A few hours' rest has done you good, hasn't it? Or has the fever come back?" Luke made a show of feeling Skye's forehead.

"Sorry, Sir. I don't seem to be able to control my brain to mouth connection this evening." Skye took a big gulp of chocolate. If he was drinking, he wasn't speaking and that seemed like a wise move, though Luke was unperturbed, his expression unreadable as usual.

"I think being ill has thrown you. You'd only just started getting used to your routine then it all went out of the window. Routine is a form of security. Psychological bondage, if you like."

Skye thought about that for a moment. "You're right, Sir. I like to know what I have to do and when. I tend to panic without those boundaries, like I can't keep my thoughts together. They keep dashing off in different directions and that gives me a headache!" He gripped his mug. "It's better when I'm with you, Sir."

"Because I give you a focus. It's why you respond so well to chastity — which some submissives hate by the way — because it's an element of my control you have no choice but to carry with you. Taking your choices away eases your mind."

"That's exactly it, Sir! I wasn't sure how to express it. The cage…and the collar…they make me feel safe. Like you're right there with me. I must be some kind of freak. Who enjoys having their bits locked up?"

"You're not a freak. You're unique and I love that about you. I think you'd be surprised about how many subs relish chastity. There's a very close relationship between pain and pleasure — and the pain doesn't have to be physical. There's a certain delicious mental torture to knowing you can't find release, however much you might want to."

Skye blinked. Luke was good at giving him a fresh perspective on submission. He was also turning him on.

"You're still learning, still finding your way. It's my job to guide you toward being the kind of submissive you want to be."

They were interrupted by Tor, who entered the room hefting a cloth-covered tray.

"Sandwiches for supper. Can't stop, I'm afraid. The guests are heading to the dungeon for dinner and we're going to be full speed ahead for the next few hours." He deposited the tray on a nearby table.

"Go! We'll bring the tray back to the kitchen once we're done." Luke stood to uncover the tray. "This is quite a feast for a quick supper." Tor had already gone, not waiting to be thanked. Skye had guilt pangs for not being there to help with the dinner. He couldn't imagine eating anything while his friends were hard at work, but Luke handed him a loaded plate.

"I know you feel bad about not being downstairs with the others, but I want you to rest until tomorrow. If you get sick again because you go back to work too soon, Tor will have my hide."

"I hadn't thought of it like that." The sandwiches did look good, and they were Skye's favorite—brie and cranberry. He should have known that Tor would never settle for plain cheese and pickle. Skye took a bite, then another and before he knew it he was staring at a crumb-strewn plate.

"There are more," Luke said. "Or there's a plate of sliced fruit."

"Can I get you anything, Sir?" Skye took another sandwich for himself and some orange segments.

"Some of those black grapes, please."

Skye selected the plumpest grapes from the bunch then handed them to Luke on a small plate. A yawn escaped before he could stop it.

"I think you need an early night."

"Yes, Sir." Skye nibbled his sandwich. He was almost full, but he managed to finish it. The orange segments proved to be sweet and succulent. "I haven't done anything useful all day, so I don't know why I'm so tired."

"Your body has been working hard to regain its energy. It will be a few days before you're back to a hundred percent."

"But I can go back to work tomorrow...please, Sir?"

Luke gave him a stern look. "Yes, providing you eat proper meals, drink plenty of water and rest when you can. I catch you doing anything else and you won't enjoy your punishment."

Skye gulped and resolved to be good. He didn't want to find out what that punishment might be. He rubbed at his eyes.

"That's it. Bed." Luke got to his feet. "I'll deal with the tray later."

Skye wished that being ordered to bed could have happened under sexier circumstances. As it was, all he wanted to do was sleep — but he still wanted to do that with Luke rather than in his own, lonely bedroom.

When they walked passed the door to the dungeon, raucous laughter and music floated from the stairwell.

"Sounds like everything's going well down there," Luke observed. "No doubt we'll hear all about it in the morning." He led the way upstairs to the staff wing, pausing outside his door.

"Well, good night, Sir." Skye took a few steps down the corridor.

"Where do you think you're going?" Luke's question stopped Skye in his tracks. "You sleep in my room from now on, where I can keep an eye on you."

"I…yes, Sir." Joy and trepidation made Skye's heart beat faster.

"And there's no need to get anxious. All we'll be doing tonight is sleeping."

Skye couldn't remember how he'd arrived in Luke's room the previous evening. He wanted to memorize every second of his first proper night in Luke's bed. Being sick didn't count.

"You'll find a fresh toothbrush in the cupboard over the sink. You can use my toiletries and we'll move your things in here tomorrow. Go and do what you need to in the bathroom while I sort out a few things downstairs. I'll be back by the time you're done."

Having had a shower earlier in the day, Skye just freshened up and cleaned his teeth, listening out for the sound of Luke's return. When the door clicked, he padded into the bedroom barefoot and wearing just his jeans, arms full of his discarded clothes.

"Just put them on the chair for now. We'll sort out wardrobe and drawer space tomorrow." Luke stood at the foot of the bed, collar in his hand. "This has been off your neck for quite long enough. From now on, you don't take it off without my permission. The one exception is if I'm not with you and you want to take a shower or go for a swim. The leather won't do well in the water, so you can take it off yourself then, but only if I'm not around to do it for you."

Skye sighed as the collar closed around his neck and something inside him settled into place.

"Take the rest of your clothes off and kneel on the bed." Luke fetched something from the dresser that glinted when the light hit it. Skye sucked in a breath and worried that expressing an appreciation of chastity may have been short-sighted. He stripped then clambered onto the bed facing Luke.

"Knees apart, hands behind your back, keep your eyes on mine."

Skye had no idea how Luke planned to fit the chastity cage when Skye's cock was ramrod stiff, but he did as he was told, a little embarrassed at how exposed the position made him. Luke placed the chastity device on the bed before squeezing a dollop of lube onto his hand. He rubbed his palms together until they glistened then reached for Skye's erection

Breathing was no longer possible. With Luke's fingers wrapped around his cock, Skye lost the capacity for speech or thought because there was no room in his brain for anything but sensation.

"You don't come until I say you can," Luke said. Skye squeezed his eyes shut, keeping as still as he possibly could. "Open your eyes, Skye. I want you to look at me."

Skye's breath stuttered, but he met Luke's gaze. He couldn't stop the strangled moan that resulted when Luke moved his hand. A series of slow, steady pulls had Skye begging for release in seconds.

"Sir! I have to. I can't stop it. Please..."

Luke still his hand for a few moments before starting the motion again. He cupped Skye's balls in his free hand, stroking and squeezing them in time as he jacked Skye's rigid shaft. Skye panted. He sobbed his frustration, hot tears rolling down his cheeks.

"Your cock and your orgasms belong to me now," Luke growled. "Remember that."

"Yes, Sir!"

Luke slid one slick finger toward Skye's hole. "Come." He snapped the order as he rubbed his fingertip across the sensitive skin. Skye jerked, his orgasm rolling through him with an intensity that made him cry out. Sheer force of will kept his hands behind his back as he came into Luke's palm. He watched, shuddering, as Luke licked some of the seed from his fingers. "You taste good."

"I…" Skye had no idea what to say to that.

"Stay exactly as you are." Luke went into the bathroom for a few moments. Skye took some deep trembling breaths. He gripped his left wrist with his right hand, fingers digging in hard enough that he guessed he might have bruises in the morning. The slight pain helped clear his head.

Luke returned with a washcloth. He made sure Skye was clean and dry in a way that made Skye's cheeks burn. It was such personal attention and Skye was not accustomed to another man having unfettered access to the most sensitive parts of his body.

"You shouldn't be embarrassed," Luke said as he re-fitted the cock cage. "You're mine. Every part of you."

"I know. It's all so new, Sir. I'm being stupid."

"No, you're not." Luke stroked his cheek. "I should be more aware of your inexperience. I forget sometimes… You addle my brain." He locked the cock cage. "There. Now you can't escape me. I'm around your neck. I'm holding your cock. I'm with you always, Skye."

"Thank you, Sir." Skye couldn't say anything else because Luke pressed his lips to Skye's. The kiss was thorough, possessive. It left Skye in no doubt as to who was in charge, who had control. His mind eased and all the icy slivers of worry that remained melted away.

Chapter Twelve

Skye sat bolt upright, groping for his alarm clock, but his bedside table had disappeared in the night. There was a crack of light seeping from beneath the bathroom door — which had moved from where it was supposed to be. It took a few seconds of mild panic before realization dawned.

"Luke's room. I'm in Luke's bed." Skye touched the collar around his throat for reassurance. "Oh my God, I'm in Luke's bed!" The bathroom door swung open and Luke appeared, framed by the light.

"Good morning, Skye. I'm sorry if I woke you. I'm just getting ready to go out for a run, but it's still early. You should go back to sleep."

"What time is it?" Luke's running gear was very fitted and Skye needed a distraction as his cock tried to plump in its cage.

"Just after five. I usually go out about now, run for forty-five minutes or so and come in for a shower before breakfast. I should have warned you I was an early riser."

"That sounds very…energetic, Sir." Skye yawned. Rain pattered against the window panes and he didn't envy Luke his trip into a wet, cold predawn morning. "You're going to get soaked."

Luke chuckled. "Running is not for everyone, but I enjoy it. It gives me a bit of thinking time before the chaos of the day and I'm not afraid of a bit of mud and water." Skye didn't think Luke was afraid of anything. He watched while Luke laced his running shoes. "What kind of exercise do you enjoy? You can always use the pool when it's not full of guests."

"I don't swim, Sir." In his drowsy state, Skye almost gave Luke a detailed explanation of that statement but clamped his mouth shut at the last minute. The knowing look in Luke's eyes told him that he wouldn't be able to remain silent on the subject forever but for now, he was getting a free pass because Luke moved to the door.

"I'll see you at breakfast. Get some more rest."

He left and Skye flopped onto his back for a luxurious stretch. He felt much better. He was still a little tired, but the headache had gone and there was no trace of nausea. There was no way he was ever going to get back to sleep, so he headed into the bathroom for a hot shower.

Washed, brushed and dressed Skye made his way to the kitchen just before six o'clock. The next hour passed in a blur as he caught up with his friends, reassuring them that he was better and brushing off their requests for him to sit down and take a break. Luke returned, flushed and damp-haired from the shower, and took his seat at the head of the table. Every now and again his penetrating gaze would reach Skye, sending pleasurable shivers down his spine.

"I hope you had a good run, Sir." Skye spoke in a brief moment of calm.

"You're completely mad going out in this weather," Tor observed. "Give me a nice dry gym any day."

"Each to his own," Luke replied. "It was refreshing, thank you, Skye. You'd be welcome to come with me on another day."

"That's kind of you, Sir." Skye scrambled for an excuse not to accept the offer. "But I think I'd slow you down too much."

"Nice save, Skye." Tor grinned.

Once the meal was over and the dishes cleared away, Luke asked Rayne and Tor to stay behind. He placed a fresh copy of the contract on the table.

"Skye and I would like you both to act as our witnesses. Now seems to be as good a time as any." He laid a silver fountain pen on the table before pulling Skye onto his lap.

"No doubts or reservations from either of you?" Tor asked.

Skye shook his head, trying not to bounce with excitement.

"None." Luke wrapped both his arms around Skye's waist. Tor signed the papers then pushed them across to Rayne.

"Aw, you two are so cute together I can't bear it." Rayne scrawled his signature without hesitation. "There, now you're official. Congratulations!"

Tor leaned across the table to shake Luke's hand. He gave Skye a wink. "For once, I'm in agreement with the imp. Congratulations to both of you and good luck, because now the hard work begins."

Skye snuggled against Luke's chest. He wasn't afraid of hard work and he was prepared to do whatever he had to, to make a go of things.

"Thank you both," Luke said with a rare smile. "We have a business to run and guests to please." He lifted Skye from his lap and gave him a gentle kiss. "When you're done with the guests' breakfast I want you to take a rest for a while, even if you just sit in the snug with a book for an hour."

"Yes, Sir." Skye suspected that Luke would be checking up on him.

"I'll make sure he takes a break," Tor said, grinning. "I've got a bottle of water in the fridge for you too. You need to keep drinking while you're working. If you feel thirsty, then it's too late and you'll be heading back toward dehydration again."

"Good advice," Luke said as he left the kitchen. "Make sure you follow it, Skye."

"I will. I don't want to get sick again."

"None of us want that!" Rayne piped up. "This place isn't the same without you around." He caught Tor's eye. "I know, I know...get my cute little butt to the garage. I'm going."

"Less cute, more in need of another spanking," Tor murmured on his way to the kitchen.

Skye smiled, glad that everything was back to normal.

* * * *

The guests' breakfast meant another round of explanations and gratitude for their well wishes. Skye would have liked to hide in the kitchen, but everyone arrived at once and it was all he could do to keep up with the demand for Tor's cooking. The entire tribe was heading to the dungeon for the day to follow through with some plot they had cooked up at dinner the night before. Fergus and Henry were joining them and had made sure the fridges down there had been well stocked with bottled water and juices.

Once he had cleared, Skye thought he'd be safe until he needed to set up for lunch, so he made his way to the snug where he found Goran pottering around behind the bar.

"Hey, Skye. Are you here on an enforced rest break?"

Skye nodded. "I won't be in your way, will I?"

"Not at all. In fact, I'm almost done here so you can have some peace and quiet. I'm going to hit the gym to work off some of Tor's calories. The guests are all in the dungeon, aren't they?"

"Yes, they went down en masse while I was clearing the breakfast things." Settling in a chair near the bookcases, Skye scooped the local newspaper off the table in front of him to have a browse. He wasn't in the mood for anything heavy. Serving breakfast had worn him out more than he had expected.

The main news story was about a tractor shedding its load of turnips across a main road, causing traffic chaos. It didn't get more exciting than that, but Skye found it soothing to read about the everyday goings-on in the villages dotted in and around the forest. He scanned the vacancies page, curious to see what kind of work opportunities there were. Most ads seemed to be for retail positions or for a range of roles in hotels and guesthouses. One listing caught his eye, though.

Researcher/historian required for ongoing projects. Can be home-based. Some local travel required. Email for further information.

Then it gave an email address. Skye nibbled on his lower lip, wondering what the projects might be about, the description was so vague. It wouldn't hurt to send an email, but he would ask Luke about it first. He had a job, after all, and had no intention of letting anyone down so soon after starting at The Retreat.

The room was warm and a shaft of sunlight fell across Skye's body. Goran had departed without him noticing and now his eyelids drooped. He let them close thinking that it would do no harm to doze for a while. It was quiet in the snug, far enough away from other parts of the house that sound didn't travel. He drifted into a state where he wasn't asleep but not quite awake either. He could picture Tor, Benjy and Frank working away in the kitchen, Goran roaming the wine cellar, Fergus and Henry getting up to Lord knew what in the dungeon with their guests, Rayne tinkering in the garage and Luke working in his office. In Skye's imagination, Luke's hair was tousled, his dark-rimmed spectacles balanced on his nose. He had no shirt on and wore tight leather trousers rather than his usual smart slacks. Skye chuckled. Luke in leather would be a dream come true. It might not be realistic but they were his dreams and he was entitled to populate them in any way he fancied. He shifted as his cage applied uncomfortable pressure to his cock, which had responded to his fantasies in an entirely predictable way. He unzipped his fly, slipping his hand into his underwear to fondle the metal imprisoning his dick. It had significant weight but wasn't uncomfortable. Its presence alone was enough to color his daydreams.

Gradually, he became aware of someone else in the room. A slight shift in the air, a rustle of fabric then the creak of antique furniture followed by the drift of a vanilla scent beneath his nostrils. Reluctant to let go of the pictures in his head, Skye was in no rush to open his eyes, but the pull of curiosity was too strong.

Once his sleep-blurred vision came into focus, he discovered Luke sitting in the chair next to him. "Oh! Sir... I'm sorry. I was just resting my eyes."

"From the smile on your face, I'd love to know what it was you were dreaming about... And what you think you're doing with that hand?"

Skye gasped, yanking his hand from his trousers before zipping his fly with embarrassing haste. "I wasn't asleep, Sir, just daydreaming... About you." Skye couldn't bring himself to meet Luke's gaze after such an admission. Luke placed a finger beneath his chin and tilted his head up.

"I'm glad to be so inspiring."

Flustered, Skye moved to his knees. "Is there anything I can do for you, Sir?" He fixed his eyes on the bulge in Luke's trousers.

Luke stroked his hair. "Only if you want to."

Skye couldn't imagine anything he wanted more. He nuzzled Luke's thigh before reaching for his zipper with trembling fingers. Nervous as he was, it was still just the work of a moment to free Luke's cock, which proved to have a slight curve. Skye ran his fingers from root to tip in reverence, memorizing every ridge and vein. Luke shifted, parting his legs wider to give Skye better access. Skye in turn shuffled on his knees to get closer.

"Hands behind your back," Luke growled. "I really need to get into the habit of carrying handcuffs with me."

Skye clasped his hands behind his back, lacing his fingers together in tight formation so he didn't forget Luke's order in the heat of the moment. He peeked at Luke from beneath his lashes, seeking permission to continue. Luke's brief nod was all he needed.

First, Skye circled the plump head of Luke's cock with his tongue, letting the flavor settle on his taste buds. He breathed deeply, taking in Luke's unique scent — not wanting to deny any of his senses. Above him, Luke grumbled. He twined his fingers in Skye's hair, tugging him closer. Skye let Luke guide him, taking his shaft into his mouth, enjoying the solid weight on his tongue. Luke didn't force him or try to make him take more than he was ready for.

Relaxing, Skye steadied his breathing and ducked his head. He gagged a little, recovered, then tried again, taking Luke as deep as he could. He sucked hard, relishing the sensation of his lips pressing into Luke's soft skin to find the hardness beneath. He lapped at the head before dipping forward again. This time, Luke held him in place for a few seconds before allowing him to move. Skye, trusting that Luke would never push him too hard too soon, focused on applying pressure with his lips. Luke's cock still hadn't reached his throat.

Next time. Skye put all his concentration into giving Luke pleasure. He sucked and licked until his jaw ached and when Luke pushed deep into his throat, he swallowed. It was such a strange sensation, but he had no time to think about it because Luke's muscles tensed. His grip on Skye's hair tightened. Seconds later he came, his seed coating Skye's tongue in salt-sweet heat.

Skye stayed where he was, waiting for Luke to loosen his hold. He lapped at his shaft and listened as Luke sighed with satisfaction. Skye knew how he felt, his own rush of pleasure when Luke came was as great as if he had orgasmed himself. His whole body warmed with the knowledge that he had brought his Dominant to release. The ache as his dick attempted to swell in the chastity device nudged at the edges of his awareness, but it didn't detract from his attention, which was entirely on Luke. A slight tug on his hair told Skye he could move. He knelt back on his heels and raised his eyes to meet Luke's, anxious to see some sign that he had pleased him.

Luke's face was flushed, his eyes bright and he smiled. He tucked his dick away and tidied his clothes before patting his lap. "I'd guess we have some time before any of the guests appear for the pre-dinner drinks."

Skye scrambled into his lap, relaxing into Luke's hold. He was glad Luke had nothing against cuddling. He had heard that some Dominants didn't allow it and he couldn't imagine being in a relationship with somebody like that. He craved close contact with Luke like an addiction.

"That was wonderful, Skye, thank you. Please believe that it was not my intention to seduce you, but when I saw you dozing in the armchair... So sweet and peaceful..."

"It was my pleasure, Sir."

"Still, I promise to be more controlled in future. Anyone could have walked in on us."

Skye let the idea of people watching them play out in his head. To his surprise, it didn't bother him as much as he thought it would.

"Do I have a trainee exhibitionist on my hands?" Luke asked, apparently interpreting his expression and coming to an accurate conclusion.

"I don't think so, Sir. It's just that there wasn't room in my head for anyone but you so, if people had been watching, I don't think I'd even have noticed."

Chuckling, Luke stroked his hair. "Something for us to discuss if the occasion ever arises, though I think it's safe to say that I'd much rather keep you to myself."

They sat in comfortable silence for a while, the only sounds the ticking of the mantel clock and the distant rustle of wind in the trees. Skye had no desire to move but when the clock struck eleven, he knew he had to get back to work.

"Sir…"

"Yes, I know. Time to get back to the real world. Once you're done with lunch service today, you'll join me in my office for the afternoon."

On the surface, the invitation was innocuous but there was something in Luke's tone that promised… Skye shook his head. His imagination was running away with him. "Yes, Sir." He got to his feet, but Luke pulled him back for a kiss. When he let Skye go, Skye had to clutch the arm of the chair for balance.

"Now you may go."

Skye drifted toward the kitchen in a daze and it was only when he banged the door frame with his hip that he gave himself a shake. He needed to get his head back where it was needed, on crockery and glassware, rather than the firm press of Luke's lips.

* * * *

Luke tapped his pen against his notepad, his mind on far more enjoyable things than future bookings. He'd not planned for the way things had turned out in the snug before lunch, but the trip to check on Skye's wellbeing had turned into a memorable treat. He had spent a good half an hour afterward debating his behavior, wondering if he had taken advantage of the situation. It had been impossible to resist the pleading in Skye's violet eyes and his earnest focus on giving Luke the best blow job he'd ever had, melted Luke's heart. Skye had no thought for his own pleasure and hadn't even hinted with so much as a look that Luke should reciprocate in any way. He'd relaxed into Luke's arms as if all his ambitions for the day had been achieved. Luke could have stayed there, Skye's slender body pressed to his, for the rest of the day and been quite contented. Sometimes the demands of the real world were a pain in his arse.

Lunch had been a quick sandwich and an apple, eaten at his desk. He had checked in to the banqueting hall, had a quick chat with Roy and Saul, then left as most of the others were taking short breaks from the dungeon to grab a bite. There was no regular schedule and Skye was busy serving those who did appear so Luke hadn't wanted to distract him. There would be time enough to enjoy his submissive later in the day. He was keen to discuss what Skye had been dreaming about, because his expression had been intriguing to say the least. Knowing that the daydream had been about him sparked his curiosity even more.

He checked his watch for the fifth time, wondering how long it would be before Skye was able to join him, then laughed at his own behavior. Skye had him tangled in knots only a few hours after signing their contract. He got back to reviewing forthcoming bookings, knowing that he would have to write out to those on the waiting list soon—no cancellations had arisen and The Retreat was booked solid for the next eighteen months. He had plans to offer a service in future for men who were willing to share their booking when they weren't using all the bedrooms. It would reduce the considerable cost and perhaps alleviate the disappointment that came with the long waiting times. There would have to be a careful matching process to ensure people were compatible, but Luke was sure he could make it work. He needed to discuss the plan with Carey but didn't doubt that he would gain his support.

His remaining concentration was shredded by a pounding on his office door, which opened before he could say anything. Henry appeared, bare-chested and white-faced.

"Mr. Redding, can you come, sir? It's Fergus…he's hurt."

Luke was already on his feet. He didn't bother asking for more information, choosing instead to go and see for himself. Henry was excitable but wasn't one to exaggerate. If he said Fergus was hurt, there was no doubt it was true. There was a sizeable first aid kit in the dungeon so Luke went straight there. He found Fergus, even paler than Henry, resting against the spanking bench. He was trembling, head down. Saul had an arm around his shoulders and a few of the other guests were gathered around.

"Luke, I'm glad you're here. I can't tell you how sorry I am that this has happened." Roy ran up with the first aid box, placing it on the bench.

"What has happened?" Luke asked. When Fergus looked up, it was easy to work it out for himself. A nasty cut ran the length of Fergus's cheek, ending millimeters from his eye. Blood streaked his face.

"It was an accident, Mr. Redding." Fergus's voice shook.

Luke decided that dealing with the injury was more important than determining the exact course of events at that moment. He pulled on a pair of latex gloves from the medical kit before unwrapping a sterile dressing. He pressed it to Fergus's cheek.

"Hold it in place, Fergus. Press as hard as you can stand. It'll slow the bleeding." He turned to Henry, who had followed him down the stairs. "Fetch Tor, then ask Rayne to get the car ready. We need to get Fergus checked out at the hospital. Ask Skye to fetch some respectable clothes and a warm coat from Fergus's room — leather shorts will cause quite a commotion in casualty." Henry dashed away. "Fergus, turn around so I can see your back."

Fergus did as Luke ordered. His back was striped with red lines, but the skin wasn't broken. "This will be fine with some salve applied. Do you have any other injuries?"

"No, Sir. I wanted this — hurt so good, you know? It was an accident."

"I have no doubt it was." Luke found some antiseptic spray. "This will sting a bit. Lift the dressing for me." He sprayed the wound, which looked clean beneath the oozing blood. "Okay, it may not need stitches, but it's best to be sure." Roy handed him a towel from the dungeon's stock and Luke put it around Fergus's shoulders. "Let's get you upstairs." As he spoke, Tor arrived. Luke gave him a short explanation. "Tor will take you to wait for Rayne and help you get dressed. I'll be there in a minute or two."

Tor took everything in then left, supporting Fergus as best he could. A large bearded man stepped forward.

"I was the one doing the demonstration," he said. "I can only apologize. My foot slipped as I stepped into the stroke and the whip curled around his cheek. He could have lost his eye. If there's anything I can do…" His sub clung to his side, sobbing.

"It's Aston, isn't it?" Luke asked, getting a brief nod in return. "Accidents happen. Fergus knows the risks of his job and this wasn't deliberate. I won't tell you not to feel bad because you obviously do, but let it go. Enjoy the rest of your day. Look after Sean." Aston ruffled his sub's hair. "I'll write up a report of the incident, which you can look over. This isn't the first mishap we've had down here, and it won't be the last." He tried to project reassurance. "Saul, if there's anything you need while I'm gone, please ask Goran. I'll let him know what's going on."

"I will. And let young Fergus know that we're all thinking about him."

After stripping off his gloves and grabbing two spare dressings from the first aid kit, Luke made his way back upstairs. He found Tor and Goran in the front hall where Skye was helping Fergus into a t-shirt and jumper, keeping the fabric away from his face.

"Rayne is bringing the car around," Goran said. "You're going with Fergus?"

Luke nodded. "Yes. You and Goran are needed here. I'm not sure how long it will take, so, Tor,- you get on with preparations for tonight's dinner. Goran, look after the guests. Aston in particular is shaken up and his sub is a mess — though it's clear this was an unfortunate accident."

"I'll break out the brandy. Hot toddies all round will do the trick." Goran strolled toward the snug.

"Skye, you do whatever Goran and Tor need. Go to all the guests' rooms when they're finished in the dungeon and make sure they have everything they need and keep an eye on Henry for me."

"Yes, Sir." Skye seemed calm. "Fergus will be fine, won't he, Sir?"

"I'm sure he will. Now, tonight's theme is *A Midsummer Night's Dream*. Let's make it a magical experience for everyone."

"Rayne's here." Tor held the door open while Luke escorted Fergus to the car. As he climbed in, Luke wondered if Skye was experiencing the same separation anxiety he was.

* * * *

Five hours, three cups of terrible coffee, two stitches and a dressing later, Luke got back to The Retreat. The entrance hall was empty, but faint sounds of laughter and music came from the direction of the banqueting hall. Rayne and Fergus came in behind him, chattering away.

"You can put the car away, Rayne. Fergus, I think you should go to your room and rest. I'll let everyone know that you're okay."

"Thank you for taking me to the hospital, Mr. Redding. I'm glad there wasn't any need for more than two stitches. My face is starting to come back to life now. It's sore, but not too bad."

"The nurse said it was a nice straight wound and that it shouldn't scar—but no whipping demonstrations until you're healed, okay? You should take some painkillers too."

"But I enjoy it, Mr. Redding. The heat and the ache…" Fergus gave a little shiver. "So good."

"There speaks a true pain slut." Luke sighed. "I'll see if someone's free to help you salve your back. No arguing, you need to take care of yourself whether you like the pain or not. Remember—don't get that dressing wet tonight."

Fergus nodded. Once he had disappeared toward the staff wing, Luke went into his office and took a few deep breaths. His patience had been tested to the limit by the congested waiting room, screaming toddlers and assorted drunks queueing for treatment at the hospital. The liquid that came out of the vending machine, which had the front to call itself coffee, had been an insult to his taste buds. He needed a few moments' peace before checking on the guests.

"Sir?"

At the sound of Skye's soft voice, Luke turned. He gaped. "Is that…body paint?"

"Yes, Sir." Skye took two steps into the office. "Is Fergus…?"

"He's fine. Two stitches and if he's careful, it shouldn't scar." Luke steadied himself against the desk. Skye's entire body was decorated in swirling designs of silver, green and blue. His hair was gelled into spikes and his face was made up with glitter and jewels. At first glance, he could have been naked beneath the paint, but careful study revealed flesh-colored shorts under the decoration. "You are…stunning."

Skye ducked his head. "Thank you, Sir. Henry and I helped each other. The guests love it."

"I'm sure they do!" Luke loosened his collar.

"We're supposed to be fairies in Oberon and Titania's court. The guests have made incredible efforts with their own costumes and the banqueting hall looks fabulous. Tor and the boys created this amazing feast — it all looks so decadent and luxurious. There's gold food paint and glitter everywhere." Skye giggled, the sound sending a shiver of desire down Luke's spine. "I've no idea how long it's going to take me to get all this paint off and I don't think my hair will ever be the same again."

Luke debated his options. Jump in the swimming pool fully clothed. Run upstairs and take an ice-cold shower. Bend Skye over the desk right there and then. Or be professional and check in with the guests. His heart approved of the desk option, his body needed the shower option, but his head gave him a mental smack then went with professional. He sighed. Being the boss was sometimes a pain in the behind.

"Why don't you show me? I'll bring the camera and, if the guests don't mind, I'll take a few pictures."

"They've been snapping away all evening, Sir," Skye said. To Luke's surprise Skye held out his hand. Luke took it and found himself pulled toward the banqueting hall. He followed Skye's lead, in danger of stumbling over his own feet as his eyes were fixed on Skye's lithe, glittering body. The image would be fodder for his dreams for a long time to come.

As soon as he entered the banqueting hall, Luke was assaulted by a barrage of questions about Fergus's well-being. Even Sean, Aston's shy sub, found the courage to approach him. He gave all the appropriate reassurances, letting them know that Fergus would be back on duty in the morning. There were exclamations over the need for two stitches before the conversation descended into discussions of everyone's hospital experiences. When various scars were revealed, Luke decided it was time to make his exit. He got Saul's permission to take a few pictures, assuring him that any he used would not show faces, then retreated to the staff room. Tor, Benjy and Frank were seated around the table with their usual pot of tea, all looking worn-out and frazzled. Luke had to repeat his story again while Tor poured him a mug of tea.

"It has been quite an evening," Tor said. "We've served dessert and we're fitting in a quick break before coffee and sweets. Everything's prepared and ready to go. Skye and Henry will come and collect them when they think it's time."

"Everything out there looks spectacular. This bunch really take their costumes seriously, don't they?"

"I think they're one of the best groups we've ever had. Maybe it's the air in Manchester, but they're all very amenable. We've not had a single complaint about anything. They're polite and respectful to the staff and it's clear they care for one another. I think Roy and Saul set a fine example."

Luke nodded, sipping his tea. "They won't all be like this, but we haven't come across a bad bunch yet. It'll be interesting to see how they handle their slave auction tomorrow night." He chuckled. "I've a feeling the costumes will be even skimpier than tonight, though with a lot less glitter. We're going to be finding that stuff in every nook and cranny for months."

"Do you want anything to eat, sir?" Frank asked. "You missed supper. I could throw together a sandwich for you."

"Did Skye eat?"

"Yes," Tor replied. "I made sure he and Henry had sandwiches and salad before they started this evening's service. It took both of them to decorate the banqueting hall, then Benjy helped Goran with the drinks whilst Skye served the food. Goran created some amazing cocktails in different colors. They had sparklers in them and some of them even smoked with dry ice. The man's like a bartending wizard with his potions."

"Then, I will have a sandwich. Thank you, Frank. Don't go to too much trouble, I'll have whatever is on hand." Luke relaxed in his seat, impressed at how well organized everything had been in his absence. He trusted his staff, but it was always good to witness their efficiency with his own eyes. Delighted guests meant recommendations for future bookings. He wanted The Retreat to have the best reputation it could and tonight's impressive display could only help.

Over the next hour, Luke only saw Skye when he dashed in and out of the kitchen. The fleeting glimpses of glistening body paint were enough to keep Luke hard and on edge. He couldn't get it out of his head that other men were looking at what was his, even though he knew it was part of Skye's job. He sighed and poured yet another mug of tea, counting down the minutes until he could have Skye to himself.

Chapter Thirteen

"This evening was a challenge for me." Luke gazed at Skye who was kneeling at his feet, naked and clean of makeup and body paint. "I admit I was jealous that others could see you in all your ethereal beauty." Skye blushed then ducked his head. His hair, still damp from the shower, was darker than usual. "I wanted to lock you away. Keep you all to myself." The gleam of Skye's cock cage caught Luke's eye. "Of course, a part of you is already locked away." Luke refastened his collar around Skye's neck. "I should replace this with one you can get wet. Something in silver, to go with your hair." Skye shivered, his skin pinking even more.

Luke rolled the plug he was holding between his hands, warming the steel. It was smooth, tactile and weighted inside, perfect for training purposes. "Hands and knees." Skye fell forward on command, head down, arse in the air. Luke slicked the plug with lube before pressing the tapered end to Skye's hole. "Relax. You'll take this because I want you to." He pushed, taking care not to move too fast. Skye's body accepted the narrow end of the plug with ease then resisted as it widened. Luke paused, waiting for Skye to instruct his body to accept the intruder, then applied steady pressure. As Skye's channel stretched, Luke held his breath. The plug narrowed again and disappeared inside Skye's body, leaving the flat base and pull ring exposed. "Very good. Stay where you are." Luke wiped the excess lube from his hands then retrieved the cane he had left on the bed. "One stroke for your discipline tonight."

"Yes, Sir." Skye wiggled his butt in invitation and Luke had to repress a smile. He dragged the cane across Skye's bare skin before drawing his arm back. The single blow was just hard enough to leave a red mark that bloomed dark before fading to a paler shade. Luke put the cane on the dresser, signaling that discipline was over. "Are you tired?"

"No, Sir. I mean, my body is, but my mind is still jumping all over the place."

Luke fetched a towel from the bathroom then spread it over the bed. "Lie down, on your back."

Skye scrambled onto the bed. "Spread your legs, hands over your head." Luke treated himself to a thorough examination of Skye's body. He unlocked the cock cage, checking for any sore spots. but other than a few dents in the skin. there was no sign that the device was bothering Skye at all. He watched as Skye's dick went from flaccid to rigid in a matter of seconds.

"I can see parts of your body that aren't that tired." He went to the bathroom to fetch a tube of depilatory cream and the applicator. "Time to get rid of this stubble." He stroked a finger across Skye's groin, steering clear of his cock. Beneath the skin. Skye's muscles twitched. His fingers clenched and unclenched.

"I'm going to come, Sir. I have to…"

"Not until I say you can." Luke smoothed the cream around the base of Skye's cock, making sure every re-emerging hair was covered. Skye took short deep breaths, every muscle flexing.

"Keep your legs apart."

"Sir…"

"This takes about fifteen minutes to work. You need to keep still."

"I don't know if I can, Sir."

Luke slipped off his belt, made a loop then slipped it around Skye's wrists. He tied the other end to the headboard. Two silk ties from the dresser served as restraints for Skye's ankles, which Luke tied to the footboard. "I need to bring proper restraints up here."

"Yes, Sir," Skye said with a pained expression. "The cream tingles."

"I can distract you from the sensation," Luke said. He flicked one of Skye's nipples and it peaked into a hard nub. He repeated the action with the other one until the skin around it reddened and Skye was pulling on his bonds. "Have you ever thought about getting these pierced? They'd be even more sensitive. I could run a chain from here to here." He brushed his hand across Skye's chest. "Use a link chain to a cock ring. Make it short enough that it would tug every time you moved."

Skye whimpered. "You're not helping, Sir."

"Of course, we don't have to wait. The same effect can be achieved with a good set of clamps." Luke gave one of Skye's nipples a pinch. His body rippled and his hips rolled as he worked the plug in his arse.

"You could have told me you were a sadist, Sir."

"But look at how much fun you're having finding out." Luke tested a small section of the cream and the hair came away easily. "This is cooked." Using the small plastic applicator, he scraped away the cream and hair, wiping it onto some tissues. Soon Skye's groin was denuded and smooth. A dampened tissue wiped away the remains of the cream.

"There. All done." Luke took his time disposing of the equipment and washing his hands, well pleased with the results he had achieved. Skye's torment was delicious. Spread-eagled and bound, he was a feast for Luke's eyes. That he could touch and play at will sent thrills of pleasure to Luke's groin.

Without giving Skye any warning, Luke wrapped his hand around Skye's straining shaft. He rubbed his thumb over the gleaming head. Skye's body jerked and he came with a cry, pumping his release over Luke's hand.

"Oh God, oh God, oh God." He thrust into Luke's grip, which Luke tightened, providing more friction until Skye was milked dry and gasping for air.

After a lingering kiss, Luke released Skye's wrists and ankles then went to the bathroom for a shower. By the time he was finished, Skye was sound asleep. He still lay sprawled in the same position, taking up three-quarters of the bed. Luke watched him for a while, enjoying the view. Skye didn't stir when Luke locked him back in the chastity device, nor when he rearranged Skye's limbs so that he could get into bed too. Luke lay still, wakeful, imagining how it would feel to have Skye beneath him — to make love to him.

Too soon. His head told him to be patient, to give Skye time. His heart and his body had other ideas. Roy, Saul and their friends would be gone Saturday morning.

Their new guests weren't arriving until the following Monday. That meant a full day and half when they could be together without the demands of work interfering. Luke planned to keep Skye in chastity for the next thirty-six hours. Tomorrow, he'd use a bigger plug. When the time came, he wanted Skye ready for him. He turned onto his side and straight away Skye wriggled to press against him. Luke sighed. His willpower wasn't limitless.

* * * *

The guests are making the most of their last day, aren't they, Sir?" Skye plopped his aching body down into a chair in the snug. "I'm worn out."

"They know how to have a good time, that's for sure." Luke peered over the top of his book, glasses balanced on the end of his nose. Skye's heart gave a little jump. "How did lunch go?"

"Delivered to five different places. The dungeon, three bedrooms and the gym. I've never seen exercise equipment used that way before, Sir."

"Do I want to know?"

"Best not. Suffice to say, Henry was getting quite a work-out and his grin was bigger than a Cheshire cat's."

Goran, who was polishing glasses behind the bar, gave a low chuckle. "The current houseboys are enthusiastic about their roles, aren't they? Their dedication is admirable."

Skye snickered. "Is yesterday's local paper still here?" He rummaged through a pile on the table. "Yes! Here it is." He rifled through the pages.

"Something interesting in there?" Luke asked. "Other than turnips, that is."

"I wanted to show you… Here it is." Skye folded the page back then handed the paper to Luke. "It's the small ad for a researcher. I wanted to get your opinion on whether I should email for more information." Skye bounced on his chair, eager to hear Luke's thoughts.

"There can't be any harm in it. I think I recognize that email address. Hold on." Luke pulled out his phone. "B Doring at Rydings dot com…yes, here it is." He handed the phone to Skye. "I don't know Brenda Doring in person, but she's a respected academic with a slew of books to her name. I've read a couple of them — she specializes in maritime history, with a particular interest in shipwrecks."

"Wow." Skye scrolled through the Wikipedia page. "She dives herself, too."

"Rydings is the name of her house. It's a wedding venue, hence the dot com. It's in one of the villages on the far side of Lyndhurst, I think. You should use the computer in my office to take a look. I'm sure there'll be a website."

"Does that mean you're okay with me getting in touch, Sir?"

"Of course. You didn't have to ask me…but I'm glad you did."

Skye couldn't imagine doing such a thing without Luke's permission. "Thank you. I mean…I'm sure Professor Doring will be looking for someone with a lot more experience than me, but I don't lose anything by emailing her, do I?"

"No, and sometimes the smallest things turn into the biggest opportunities. Would you like to take a look now? We have some time before set-up for the auction starts."

"Can't wait to see how that turns out," Goran chimed in. "I have my gladiator costume ready and waiting."

"Sounds hot!" Skye exclaimed, nibbling his lip when he caught Luke's scowl. Goran's belly laugh echoed around the room.

"You're in big trouble now, boy." Still chortling, he made for the door. "I'm heading out for an hour—need some fresh air before tonight's shenanigans begin. All this hotness needs to be in tip-top condition." He winked then closed the door behind him.

Skye raised his eyes to meet Luke's piercing gaze. He gulped.

"Calling another man hot in front of your Dom, even if it's true, is not appropriate, young man." Luke patted his lap. "Trousers down. Over my lap."

"Sorry, Sir." More excited than nervous, Skye unzipped his jeans. He pushed them and his underwear down his thighs. With hindsight, he should have moved closer to Luke first because now he had to waddle over to him. He tipped himself over Luke's lap. His toes scraped the floor and his caged cock nestled in the space between Luke's thighs. Blood rushed to his head.

He expected the sting of a blow but instead, Luke stroked his arse.

"So beautiful and all mine. You do understand that, don't you, sweetheart?"

"Yes. Sir. Yes! Want to be yours, no one else's." Skye squirmed under Luke's gentle touches.

"Good, because tomorrow I'm going to take this gorgeous arse. No more waiting." Luke pulled Skye's cheeks apart then brushed a finger over his hole. "I'm going to fill you and fuck you so there's no room in your head for anything or anyone, but me."

Skye gasped as Luke pushed a fingertip inside him.

"And now I'm going to spank you so that this evening, and tonight, every time you move you'll think of me."

In its cage, Skye's cock attempted to swell. He moaned, desperate for more. Luke patted his behind then gave him six hard strokes, targeting the sensitive junction between arse and thigh. When he was done, he rested a hot palm on the small of Skye's back.

"All over."

"Thank you, Sir." Skye took a few deep, heaving breaths. When Luke allowed it, he slid to his knees, resting his head on Luke's thigh. Now the distraction of pain had gone, thoughts whirled around his head. There was so much to think about, it was overwhelming. Foremost was that he had spoken without thinking and even though there was no doubt that Goran dressed as a gladiator would be hot as hell, he shouldn't have said it out loud. Luke had spanked him as punishment, but it had been one of the most erotic experiences of his life.

The touches, the ache, just the position over Luke's lap — if it hadn't been for the cage, he was sure he would have come. He could still feel where the tip of Luke's finger had penetrated his channel. He wanted Luke inside him with an all-consuming need and unless his imagination was playing tricks on him Luke had said that it was his intention to fuck him. Tomorrow. And it had sounded as if Luke was just as impatient as he was for them to be together. Skye rubbed his cheek on the soft fabric of Luke's trousers. His hair got a tug.

"Get dressed, Skye. You'll be spending the rest of your free time this afternoon with me in my office."

"Yes, Sir." Skye got to his feet, hampered by the jeans and underwear that were still around his knees. He adjusted his clothing, giving Luke a tentative smile. His reward was a deep, aggressive kiss that left him even more befuddled than he had been before. He followed Luke back to his office, grateful for the opportunity for some thinking time.

Luke took the seat behind his desk, put his elbows on the wooden surface and steepled his fingers. The office door was closed, but not locked.

"I imagine there's a lot going on in your head, Skye. Some quiet time will be good for both of us. Take your clothes off, please."

Skye stripped, his mind wandering to the fact that he wouldn't need much of a clothes budget in future, he spent that much time naked. He smiled at the thought, which was random and had come out of nowhere.

"I'm glad you're finding this amusing," Luke said, his expression stern. "No kneeling today. You may take the other chair."

Sinking into the cushioned leather, Skye made himself comfortable.

"Spread your legs."

Luke seemed to find the view of Skye's bare body and shiny cock cage intriguing, because for a few minutes he just sat and stared. Skye fidgeted, uncomfortable under his scrutiny, hoping he passed muster. Luke slid open a desk drawer. He pulled out several objects, a blindfold, what looked like a gag, several short lengths of rope and a metal chain with some kind of clip on either end.

Luke pushed his chair back and stood, his movements as smooth and controlled as always. Skye envied his certainty. "You need time to think and I'm going to give it to you," Luke said. He used two pieces of rope to bind Skye's wrists to the arms of the chair, and two more went farther up his arms. "I'm not going to tie your ankles. I want you to hold that position with your legs spread wide."

"Yes, Sir." Skye shifted a little. He wasn't uncomfortable, but it was difficult to keep his body still when his mind was so active.

"Removing any visual stimulation will help you." Luke tied the blindfold around Skye's head, cutting off the light. Not even the smallest glimmer penetrated the dense fabric. Something rubbery pressed against his lips. Skye opened his mouth and it was filled with a hard, bulbous shape that narrowed at the base, allowing him to close his mouth around it. A strap went around his head which Luke buckled, holding the gag in place.

"This kind of gag won't hurt your jaw as much as a ball gag would. Breathe through your nose. You should be able to swallow normally. Nod if you can."

Skye suckled the rubber, getting used to the taste. Swallowing wasn't a problem. He ducked his head, letting Luke know that he was okay.

"Good. Now, something to help you focus."

Skye jerked as his nipples were flicked until they burned.

"These clamps aren't the most painful type, but they will make you ache." A sharp pinch followed the cold contact of metal. Skye sucked in his breath as best he could around the gag as the bite of pain sent bolts of lightning straight to his cock. When the second one was applied, he moaned. "If you want to use your safe word, just nod your head. I'll be right here and I won't leave you."

Various soft sounds told Skye that Luke had resumed his seat behind the desk. The rustle of fabric and a creak of leather was followed by the tap of fingers on keys. The sound was soporific. Skye drifted, aware of the ache caused by the nipple clamps but not bothered by it. He clenched his arse, wishing he were plugged. The thought sent his mind to fantasies about what else would soon be filling him and a sense of happy contentment washed over him. He drifted. He could trust Luke to take care of him, to give him what he needed. He had no doubt that when his Dominant, his Luke, made love to him, every second would be perfect.

Chapter Fourteen

Time in Luke's study had given Skye a chance to clear his head. He was glad to be rid of the gag, which had left a funny taste in his mouth. His nipples still ached from the clamps and the memory of the shocking pain when Luke had taken them off would stay with him for quite a while. He'd had no idea that their removal would be so agonizing compared to having them attached. Next time — because he was sure there would be a next time, having seen the glee in Luke's eyes — he'd make sure to have some ice cubes to hand. He worried that he'd enjoyed the experience a bit too much but then dismissed the thought. Moderate pain was one of his kinks. Luke was helping him realize that.

Reenergized, he'd bounced through dinner service and was now looking forward to the slave auction. Dinner had been an amazing, decadent feast. Saul had dressed as a Roman emperor, complete with crown, while Roy had donned a golden toga. Goran had drawn admiring, lustful glances in his gladiator get-up, complete with leather skirt, and the other guests seemed to have taken their inspiration from episodes of *Spartacus*, the Doms wearing almost as little as their subs.

In celebration of the last evening of a memorable week, Fergus and Henry had forgone costumes and were parading around in nothing more than cock rings, collars and sandals. They seemed to be enjoying every moment of the attention they were getting as a result. Skye was glad he hadn't been asked to do the same. He'd fastened the strip of cloth he'd been provided with around his hips with several safety pins to ensure the knot didn't give way at an inconvenient moment. Underneath, other than the chastity device, he was naked. Bending over had to be done with extreme care.

Goran had helped Fergus and Henry with the decorations and they'd produced a small stage for the auction offerings to stand on. Bidding would be done with a mixture of chocolate coins and Monopoly money, with Goran acting as auctioneer. Skye's job was to keep the bidders supplied with snacks and drinks.

As the 'sale' commenced, Skye couldn't stop laughing. Various incentives were offered alongside the monetary bids, ranging from jelly beans to flavored lube and fluorescent rubber cock rings. The event descended into a cheerful, hysterical riot as each Dom 'won' his own sub and appropriate gratitude was received. To Skye's surprise, Rayne appeared, wearing wrist and ankle cuffs and a pink thong. Not very authentic, but no one seemed to care. Goran announced a secret bid had been received and Tor, still in his chef's whites, appeared to claim his prize. Rayne's grin spoke volumes as he was hoisted over Tor's shoulder and carried toward the kitchen.

Fergus and Henry were the final, star lot. Offering themselves as a pair, bidding was heated, but they went to Roy and Saul, which was no surprise to Skye or anyone else. With the auction over, the various couples drifted toward their rooms determined to enjoy the last few hours of their break. Skye leaned against the wall, taking in the chaos that he had to clear before he could set up for breakfast. Everyone else was occupied, so he faced the task alone.

"I think they all enjoyed themselves, don't you?"

"Luke!" Skye had no idea how his Dom managed to move so quietly. "Sir…were you watching?"

"In the background, yes. You did an excellent job. I'm proud of you." Luke pulled Skye against him so that Skye's back was pressed to Luke's front. He stroked Skye's belly before slipping a hand beneath his scanty costume to cup his arse. "Watching you move, knowing you were bare under here, I wanted to touch."

"I…" Skye's knees shook as Luke stroked between his legs, touching his balls, the soft skin behind them, the edge of his hole. "Sir…please."

"Soon, sweetheart. Tonight I'm going to chain you to my bed, plug you, play with you. Tomorrow, you're mine."

"Already yours, Sir." Skye's senses overloaded. He pressed back against Luke's body, needing to be held close.

"Indeed." Luke kissed his neck. "I'll help you clear. I get you to myself quicker that way."

Skye worked on autopilot as he made trip after trip to the kitchen. There was no sign of Rayne or Tor. Benjy and Frank were clearing up, but focused on getting finished too. Skye decided that he'd get up early to lay for breakfast. All he wanted to do at that moment was be alone with Luke.

"Are we done?" Luke poked his head around the kitchen door.

"Yes, Sir." Skye scampered toward Luke's out-held hand.

"Good night, boys. Magnificent performance again this evening." Luke still took the time to compliment Benjy and Frank. "Get yourselves to bed."

"Yes, Mr. Redding. We'll be done in a few minutes," Benjy said, plunging his cloth into a sink of steaming water. "Can't skimp. Tor is…"

"Demanding? Yes, I know." Luke grinned. "We'll see you both in the morning."

Holding Skye's hand tight, he tugged him all the way to the staff corridor—not that Skye needed any persuasion. Once they were inside Luke's room, Skye let out a sigh of relief. It had been an exhausting evening and he hadn't realized how much tension had built up in his shoulders.

"This barely merits the description of costume." Luke fiddled with the safety pins before tugging the cloth from around Skye's waist. "Oh, that's much better."

Skye kicked off his sandals, leaving him clad in his collar and chastity cage. He dropped to his knees, spreading his thighs wide, and clasped his hands behind his back.

"Very pretty."

To Skye's astonishment, and delight, Luke stripped to bare skin. He had the kind of muscle definition that Skye could only dream of, but wasn't bulky. Skye guessed that all the running kept him lean. There was enough hair on his chest that Skye wanted to rub his cheek against it. He was erect, his cock bobbing as he walked closer. Skye parted his lips, desperate for a taste.

"Not yet, love. I want you on the bed. Lie on your back."

Skye scrambled to do as he was told. Sometime during the day, Luke had fixed a set of manacles to each of the bed posts. He used them to chain Skye's wrists and ankles, stretching his body into a taut star shape. Skye hardly noticed. He was fixating on Luke's use of the word 'love'. *I'm sure it's just a figure of speech. I know I've fallen hard for him, but he's too controlled...it's too soon. I'm the emotional one.*

"I don't know what's going on in that busy head of yours," Luke said as he knelt across Skye's body. "But I'd appreciate your full attention." He crawled up the bed until he straddled Skye's head. His cock dipped tantalizingly close to Skye's lips. "What's your safe word?"

"Napoleon, Sir."

"You won't be able to use it all the time. Rattle the chains if you're unable to speak but want me to stop."

"I won't want you to stop, Sir."

Luke fucked Skye's mouth like he owned it. All Skye could do, bound as he was, was lie there and take it. He had no opportunity to be an active participant in what was happening—he had no choice but to submit to Luke's complete dominance. He relaxed his jaw and throat as best he could, ecstatic that Luke trusted himself to be so assertive. In its cage, Skye's cock tried to stiffen, the rings of metal pressing hard into his aching flesh. He gripped the chains holding his arms, clutching the metal until it dug into his palms. Luke withdrew as he came. A few drops of hot liquid splashed Skye's lips, which he licked with eager strokes of his tongue. The remainder of Luke's release hit Skye's chest and belly. Luke sat back on his haunches, panting, not resting all his weight on Skye's legs.

Still taking care of me even now. Skye beamed, jubilant that he'd been part of Luke's pleasure. He giggled as Luke ran a finger through the liquid on his chest.

"That tickles, Sir!"

"You smell of me now. I like that. If it weren't so sticky, I'd be tempted to leave you like that but as it is…" He climbed off the bed, returning with a packet of wipes that he used to give Skye a cursory clean-up. "Do you need to use an enema kit before I plug you?"

Skye's face heated. "No, Sir. I did that earlier. After I moved my things from my room."

"You can always ask me to help you with it. It's not so easy on your own."

"I manage okay, Sir." Skye couldn't imagine letting anyone be involved in such a personal activity, even Luke.

"There's no need to be embarrassed. I appreciate your forethought."

"It's a bit icky, Sir."

"A strong relationship isn't all hearts and flowers, Skye. I'm here for you whenever you need me. Icky or not." Luke smiled and his eyes lit up. He released Skye's wrists and ankles. "I'm going to use a bigger plug tonight—consider it part of your training."

"So I can take you, Sir?"

"That won't be a problem. You were made for me, but I want your first time to be as pain-free as possible. This will help." He showed Skye a ridged black rubber plug.

"Oh…that's big, Sir."

"Not as big as me. Don't worry, I'll take it slow and use plenty of lube." He coated the toy with a layer of glistening gel. "Pull your knees back."

Skye gulped. He hooked his arms beneath his knees then pulled them to his chest, hyper aware of the view Luke now had.

"You have a beautiful arse." Luke pressed the end of the plug to Skye's hole. It was cold, making him flinch. Luke stroked Skye's balls. "Perhaps a little distraction will help."

"Oh God." Skye willed his muscles to relax and the first part of the plug slipped inside him. He clenched his arse, gripping the invader, trying to push it out.

"It's not going anywhere, love. Deep breaths."

Each time Skye breathed in, Luke pushed a bit more of the plug into his channel. The stretch felt huge, but then the toy tapered.

"Well done." Luke jiggled the end of the toy, making Skye gasp. His arse muscles seemed to have developed a mind of their own, working the plug in a rhythm that made Skye drop his legs. The change in position made him gasp again. The chastity device was getting painful.

"You have no idea how perfect you look, plugged and caged for my pleasure. Do you need the bathroom before we sleep?"

Skye shook his head because speech was beyond him. He shifted to one side of the bed wondering how he would manage a wink of sleep. With the warmth of Luke's body pressed against him, his eyelids drooped.

"Sleep, Skye. That's an order."

Something in Skye's brain registered the command and he had no choice but to submit to Luke's will.

* * * *

More rested than he expected to be, Skye cruised through both the staff and guest breakfast services. Roy and Saul took the time to thank all the staff in person, even bringing Benjy and Frank from the kitchen to congratulate them on their excellent food. Fergus and Henry dealt with bringing all the luggage down to the front hall and Rayne parked the guests' cars outside the front door. Each of them had been washed and polished until they gleamed, which got new exclamations of delight as the luggage was loaded. Skye hovered in the background, helping where he could. He accepted hugs from the submissives and had his hair tousled by the Dominants more times than he could count. Fergus and Henry had standing invitations from more than one couple if they ever wanted to stay in Manchester, or even to take a short city break.

Skye had overheard Saul trying to leave sizeable tips for everyone, but Luke had turned him down, telling him that there was no expectation of that kind of reward. The Retreat paid its staff very well and excellent service was expected as a matter of course, not because anyone thought they could be earning extra money. Roy promised to email some of the photos they'd taken that they were content to be used on the website, once he'd had a chance to edit them and Luke was very happy with that arrangement.

All in all, it was a very merry bunch who headed north with promises that they would be back and that they would be recommending The Retreat to all their friends. When the cars chugged in convoy down the drive, the place seemed very empty, and for a moment the staff looked at each other, a bit lost.

Skye stood close to Luke, needing his proximity but not really understanding why.

"This is about as close to top drop as you'll get when you're working. It's like the feeling you get when you come out of subspace and the real world is still waiting. It's been an intense few days and I want you all to take time for yourselves. Relax, go out, have some fun. You'll be doing the cleaning crew a favor because they won't want you lot under their feet while they work."

Fergus and Henry retreated to their respective rooms to catch up on some much-needed sleep, making plans with Rayne to have an outing that evening to the local pub. Goran said his goodbyes as he would be heading back to London and his job at The Underground. Tor was going to travel with him as Goran had a car, because an old friend was staying in the country for a few days and he wanted to take the chance to have a short visit.

"I could do with a mug of coffee right now," Luke said. "Why don't you and I head to the snug to plan our day?" He squeezed Skye's shoulder.

"I'll make the coffee, Sir, then meet you in there." Skye was happy to have a defined task to do. That it was a job he could do for Luke made it even better. Even something as simple as providing a hot drink gave him intense pleasure.

He knew where everything was in the kitchen so it didn't take him long to brew a pot of coffee. He stacked everything he needed on a tray, along with a plate of stem ginger cookies that either Benjy or Frank must have baked earlier that morning. If he ever had time, he intended to ask them if they could teach him to cook a few simple things. He wanted to be able to bake treats for Luke by himself rather than relying on others.

He carried the tray through to the snug, placing it on a low table in front of the chair Luke had chosen. Luke's eyes were closed, his legs stretched out and crossed at the ankles, his hands behind his head. The tray clinked and he opened his eyes.

"Wonderful. Thank you, Skye. You're doing a great job of looking after me."

"You deserve it, Sir. You look tired. It's been a demanding week, hasn't it? Everybody here works so hard."

"No more than you," Luke said as he poured the coffee for both of them.

"But I don't have the same level of responsibility or all the stress that comes with it," Skye said.

"We all worry about different things, except Rayne. I don't think that boy has ever had an anxious moment in his life."

"He's a free spirit. I think he craves control though, that's why he's so attracted to Tor. They make a good couple. Rayne drives Tor mad and Tor enjoys correcting him. I think Rayne likes spankings a lot more than I do, Sir."

"You like them well enough." Luke patted his lap and for a moment Skye wondered if he was expected to lie over Luke's knees or sit on them. Either would have been fine with him.

"I just want to drink coffee and cuddle for a while. I think, after last night, I owe you some comfort time."

Skye scrambled into Luke's lap, snuggling close whilst being careful not to jiggle his drink. "I don't understand, Sir. Last night was amazing. One of the most memorable experiences of my life."

"I wasn't gentle with you. I'm afraid I lost control for a while. I hope I didn't hurt you." Luke's brow furrowed.

"You would never hurt me, Sir. I had my safe word and I know that if I'd used it you would have stopped. I'm not made of glass and I don't want you to treat me like I'm fragile. I may still be working out what I want, but you're helping me find out, and I love that."

"I think I need to send Carey and Alistair a gift basket." Luke chuckled and stroked Skye's hair. "Their plotting brought us together. They recognized what I needed and gave me you. I wanted you from the first moment I saw you crossing the dining room at The Underground. So graceful, so shy. Every man there had his eyes on you and I wanted to take you and hide you away so I could keep you all to myself. You saw a side of me last night that you'll see again. I hope that doesn't scare you."

"I can't wait, Sir." Skye petted the triangle of skin that he could get to above the top button of Luke's shirt.

"Much as I'd like to spend the entire day in bed ravishing your gorgeous body," Luke said, smiling, "I think it would be nice to spend some time together first. Would you like to go into Lyndhurst and have a walk around the shops? We could pretend to be tourists."

"That sounds wonderful, Sir. Oh, but I completely forgot, I had a response to my email to Professor Doring and she invited me to call in this morning. I was going to go back to her and say it wasn't convenient..."

"We can do that too. I can drive you there then wait in the car while you have your interview. Then we can go into Lyndhurst afterwards. Did she mention a specific time?"

"Any time before two this afternoon, Sir."

Luke munched on a cookie. "Then, as soon as I've had another one of these, we'll go." He fingered Skye's collar. "Would you like me to take this off?"

"No! It's who I am," Skye said. "She'll probably just think it's a fashion accessory anyway but if it makes a difference to her, then it's not the right job for me. Wearing your collar doesn't dissolve my brain cells. That happens when you touch me."

Luke laughed. "Good to know. No difficult questions whilst in physical contact. Got it."

Embarrassed, Skye buried his face against Luke's chest. "I need to learn to control my mouth."

"If I didn't want you to talk, I'd gag you or order you to silence."

"Is it wrong that just hearing you say that turns me on?" Skye mumbled into Luke's shirt, not expecting a response.

"Wrong in a sexy, stimulating way." Luke's husky growl made Skye whimper.

"Oh God. You know, I don't need a job. I have one. It's gonna be cold out too. We should just stay here. Cuddle under the blankets. Naked."

"Go and fetch your coat, Skye." Luke lifted him off his lap. His expression was stern, but his eyes twinkled. "You're turning into a bad influence."

As he went to fetch his coat, a warm scarf and gloves Skye decided that he didn't mind being a bad influence. He could be himself with Luke and that gave him confidence. It didn't hurt that Luke was gorgeous. Finding him in the front hall wearing a black overcoat and black leather gloves gave Skye palpitations. He added leather gloves to his fetish list alongside spectacles.

"Ready?" Luke asked.

"Yes, Sir."

"We'll have to walk around to the garages to fetch my car. I don't want to bother Rayne on his day off." He kept his arm around Skye's shoulders all the way to the converted stable block that served as The Retreat's garage. His Lexus was housed at the far end and getting into it, the smell of the leather, brought back all Skye's memories of the journey from London. It was hard to believe it had only been a week ago.

Pulling away, Luke gave him a sideways glance. "Déjà vu?"

"A little. It feels like a lifetime ago that you brought me here. I've learned so much already about what kind of submissive I want to be. I need to be. And that's thanks to you. Do you remember asking me what I was dreaming about a few days ago? I promised to tell you."

"You don't have to." Luke kept his eyes on the road, his grip firmly on the wheel.

"I dreamed about you, wearing leather," Skye snickered. "You had no shirt on. The trousers had a laced fly and you started to undo them... Then I woke up, which was so unfair."

There was a hint of pink on Luke's cheeks. "You've never seen me in leather, have you? My trousers aren't quite the way you describe them, but I'm sure I could do my best to make that particular dream come true."

All moisture evaporated from Skye's mouth. He was grateful for the chastity cage because otherwise he would be heading into a job interview with an erection. Hardly conducive to making a good impression on an esteemed academic.

Traffic was light and the drive to Rydings only took twenty minutes or so. The house was situated down a short lane in a picture-postcard hamlet. It was a beautiful property, Skye guessed Georgian in period, not massive but with extensive landscaped grounds. He could see the gazebo at one end of the garden and could well understand why it was a popular wedding venue. There was a fairy-tale quality to the setting that couldn't fail to appeal to the romantic.

His anxiety, which had been kept at bay by Luke's presence, grew exponentially once Luke had parked the car.

"I'll be waiting here when you're done," Luke said. "You'd better go in. Good luck, not that you'll need it." He gave him a quick kiss.

Gripping the car door handle, Skye hesitated. He was about to suggest to Luke that they gave the whole thing up as a bad idea when an older woman came scurrying from the direction of the house. She tapped on the car window, which Luke lowered.

"Oh my, are you Skye? That rhymes! I had it in my head that you'd be younger."

"No, Professor, I'm just the chauffeur. Skye is a little nervous to meet you."

The professor peered into the car. "No need to worry, young man, I don't bite. It's cold out here so get yourself into the house." She bustled round to Skye's side of the car and opened the door. "Your...friend can come in too, if it makes you feel more comfortable."

"Would you like me to come with you?" Luke offered.

"Yes please, Sir," Skye whispered, feeling a little ridiculous but relieved that he didn't have to be alone. He climbed out of the car to follow Professor Doring, who was already striding toward the house. She had on wellingtons, muddy trousers and a voluminous hooded jumper in a vibrant shade of purple. Her gray hair had streaks of blue scattered through it. He hurried to keep up, with Luke right behind him.

The professor led them to the side door where she kicked off her boots to reveal fluorescent yellow socks.

"Come in, come in, time's a-wasting. You wouldn't believe how much I have to do. We'll sit in the kitchen because it's the warmest room in the house at the moment. I don't bother heating the whole place when I'm the only one at home. Costs a fortune, you know."

Her relaxed manner, and running commentary, put Skye at ease. The kitchen proved to be a large airy room with a battered table in the center covered with piles of paper, an assortment of biros and colored pens and a scattering of photographs. A laptop computer, half buried, sat at one end. Skye took the chair at the other end of the table while Luke lounged against the kitchen units. Professor Doring bustled around making tea before joining him at the table after handing Luke a mug with an assessing stare. He gave her a wink, which she seemed to enjoy immensely.

When she sat, her gaze was directed at Skye's collar. He had shrugged off his coat and the shirt he wore exposed it a little. She looked from him to Luke and back again.

"Ah, I see. Good, good. You have someone to take care of you. Now, tell me a bit about yourself — the parts of your degree that you enjoyed the most."

After a shaky start, Skye relaxed into the conversation, telling the professor about his dissertation, some of the field trips he had taken and the modules he had loved the most. For the most part, she just listened, nodding and asking the occasional probing question.

"I should tell you a bit more about what I'm looking for in my assistant," she said.

"I thought the role was just for a researcher," Skye said.

"That's part of it, but what I really need is a right-hand man, or woman, to sort my life out while I'm abroad, which is around nine months of the year. My husband runs a salvage and deep sea exploration company. We have another home in the Far East and this country is way too wet and cold for my tastes now. I'm working on three different books at the moment. My publisher keeps demanding progress updates, and there are just not enough hours in the day for me to keep up with the required research and record-keeping that goes with producing accurate work. I need somebody organized, reliable and hard-working who understands how to conduct research, make detailed notes and occasionally write sections of the books, for which you would be credited of course."

Skye gaped. He couldn't believe how perfect the job sounded or that he was even being considered for it.

"Do you think you'd be interested?"

Skye asked a few more questions about the topics of the books, access to research facilities online and a few other more technical questions. "It sounds amazing," he said. "You know I have very little experience. I know in theory what to do, and I think I can do it well, but I don't have any evidence to show you other than my dissertation and a couple of articles that I wrote for the university paper."

"I'll be completely upfront with you, young man. I think you're perfect. You haven't developed any bad habits like most career academics have. You can be trained." She threw a glance in Luke's direction. "I think at first, two or three hours a day during the working week should suffice. I can email you the relevant passwords and instructions along with task lists for the week. We can Skype if you have any questions I'm quite up with all the new techno stuff you know." She quoted an hourly rate that seemed very generous to Skye. "The only other people who contacted me were either overqualified, writing their own books, or had studied subjects that were irrelevant. You're the only person I invited for an interview, so the job is yours if you want it. Do you need to talk to your…"

Luke stepped forward. "Luke Redding, Professor, Skye's partner. He makes his own decisions, I can assure you."

"Call me Sue. That's good to hear "

"Sir, I want to give it a try. I think I can work it around my responsibilities at The Retreat."

"Then you should say yes," Luke said. "We can make arrangements to ensure you have enough time."

Skye beamed. "Then I'd be very happy to accept, Sue."

Sue held up her mug. "A toast, then, to a new working relationship." Skye clinked his mug against hers, laughing. "I'm going away again next week, but I'll be in touch before then. I have your email already. Would you like me to copy in Luke on your correspondence?"

"Yes, please," Skye said. "I'd appreciate that."

Luke handed over a business card. "Here are all my contact details. You can reach Skye on these numbers as well."

"Good, good… It was a pleasure to meet you both. Do enjoy the rest of your day, I need to get back to clearing a drain in the garden. The life of a history professor is not all glamour, I can assure you." She escorted them to the door, pulled on her wellies and when they turned toward the car, she went the other way with a cheerful wave.

Back in the Lexus, Skye let out his breath in a rush. "I can't believe what just happened, Sir."

"You did a good job of telling the professor what she needed to know. She liked you and she thinks she can work with you. I'm not surprised at all. Congratulations."

"I'll make sure it doesn't affect my work at The Retreat, Sir."

"This is what you want from your career, Skye. It's important. We'll work around it and see where it goes. Now, how about we head into Lyndhurst and find a teashop that has enormous cream cakes?"

"Yes please, Sir. I could really do with something thick and creamy right now."

"You are turning into a brat," Luke said. "You've been spending too much time with Rayne."

"I don't know what you mean, Sir." Skye affected innocence but gave himself away with a giggle.

"Hmm." Luke put the car into gear then pulled away, muttering about suitable punishments and whether the dungeon would have been cleaned yet.

With a happy sigh, Skye settled into his seat feeling like he'd won the lottery.

Chapter Fifteen

"This has to be the ultimate in self-indulgent decadence," Luke said as he unbuttoned Skye's shirt. "Going to bed in the middle of the afternoon." He pulled Skye's shirt from his trousers then pushed it back on his shoulders, revealing tantalizing smooth skin and two pebbled nipples. He gave one of them a flick. "Someone's excited."

"Yes, Sir. It's been an amazing day and I've been wanting this forever. I mean, we haven't known each other that long, but ever since I can remember realizing I was a submissive, I've wanted this…for my first time to be with a kind, loving Dom who I could respect and take care of." He leaned against Luke. "You've been so patient with me."

"Respect works both ways, sweetheart. I'm honored that you've given me your trust." Luke drew him close, rubbing circles on the small of his back.

"I felt so empty when you took this plug out this morning, Sir."

"I had to force myself to go out for a run. It would have been so easy to bend you over right there and then, but I want to take my time with you. You deserve to be treated with care." He pushed a hand down the back of Skye's trousers to grip his arse. "No one else will ever get to touch this. I don't share." His tone was fiercer than he intended. Skye rubbed against him, pressing the hard metal of the chastity cage against Luke's thigh. "Enough talking." He stripped the rest of Skye's clothing with efficient movements, leaving him clad in collar, cage and a plaited leather bracelet around his wrist.

"I love my gift, Sir." Skye fiddled with the bracelet. Luke had chosen it from a selection at the craft shop they had visited because there was a thread of silver wire running through the black leather, which reminded him of Skye's hair.

"You can keep it on." Luke ran his hands over Skye's body from his shoulders, down his arms to his wrists, which he pushed behind his back and held together with one hand. With the other he cupped Skye's balls and gave them a gentle squeeze. Skye rose on his toes, giving a little squeak. Luke continued his manipulations, appreciating the warm weight of Skye's sac in his hand. He nudged him back toward the bed, only letting go when the back of Skye's legs hit the mattress. Luke dragged back the covers, rolling them to the bottom of the bed.

"I think you should undress me now."

Skye obliged with shaking hands, gripping his lower lip between his teeth as if he were concentrating on a problem. He planted kisses, unbidden, on each exposed inch of skin, dropping to his knees to lower Luke's trousers. He nuzzled Luke's erection with his cheek.

"You have a beautiful cock, Sir."

"On the bed, Skye." The tone of reprimand was not meant unkindly, but Luke knew that if Skye stayed where he was, he would come far too soon. He kicked away his trousers and underwear before climbing onto the bed to lie next to Skye. Skye was on his back, arms stretched above his head. Luke's first job was to remove the chastity cage. The key, retrieved from his trouser pocket, was already in his hand. He unlocked the device, dropping it onto the floor at the side of the bed. Skye's cock sprang to life and he moaned.

"Need to come so bad, Sir."

Luke considered tormenting him a while longer, but decided there was no harm in taking the edge off Skye's need. He was young and would recover quickly. Luke got to his knees, moistened his lips, then took Skye's rigid shaft into his mouth.

"Luke!" Skye screamed as he came seconds later. He arched his back, thrusting into Luke's mouth. Luke swallowed, then licked Skye clean. He was still semi hard.

"I'm so sorry, Sir," Skye gabbled. "I didn't mean to, I couldn't help it, you... I... Oh my God." Both his face and his groin flushed a beautiful shade of pink.

"You did exactly what I wanted you to do," Luke said, gripping Skye's shaft and jacking it a couple of times. "When I take you, I want you to be able to focus on the sensations you're experiencing rather than a desperate need to come. You've been in chastity for a long time. I'm surprised you managed to hold off long enough for me to get my mouth on you."

"That was... It was..."

"There's no need to talk," Luke said with a chuckle. "Roll onto your front."

Skye flopped onto his stomach with a sigh. Luke knelt across him and spent some time massaging his lower back and arse, digging his fingers into the tight muscles, convincing Skye's body to relax. Skye's contented moans told Luke that his efforts were worthwhile. He reached for the dispenser of lube sitting on the bedside table. He pumped some onto his fingers until they were shiny and slick before pressing one to Skye's hole. The plug had done its work, and his finger slipped into Skye's body with ease. He crooked it, brushing the tip over Skye's prostate. Skye yelped and wiggled.

"Sir!"

Luke used his free hand to give Skye's arse a smack. "Keep still." He withdrew his finger then entered Skye again using two this time. There was no resistance, just heat and the grip of Skye's inner muscles. Luke still spent some time stretching him before adding a third finger. Skye whimpered and Luke stilled.

"Am I hurting you?"

"Need more, Sir," Skye pleaded. All the preparation in the world could only help Skye so much. Luke nudged him until he rolled onto his back.

"You're sure you're happy to do this without a condom?"

"I've seen your medical records, Sir and you've seen mine… Please don't stop. Want you in me. Want to feel you, not latex."

Luke lifted Skye's calves to rest them on his shoulders. He moved into position so that the blunt head of his cock rested against Skye's glossy entrance. He added yet more lube, gritting his teeth as the urge to come became overwhelming. "Arms back over your head." Luke loomed over Skye's body, pressing his legs back. He gripped both his wrists, holding him in place, then entered him for the first time. Just an inch at first, then two. The grip of Skye's channel against his sensitive flesh was torment. Luke held still, staring into Skye's violet eyes, checking for any sign of distress. He kissed him as he pushed forward again, stealing his breath and the gasp that came with it. There was no stopping now. Luke kept pushing until he was fully seated in Skye's body.

"Burns, Sir." Skye's brow furrowed with pain. "'s good. Need you."

Slowly at first but with building speed, Luke jacked his hips until he reached a steady rhythm. His gaze was locked with Skye's and nothing in the world could make him look away. Skye was already hard again, the tip of his erection leaving wet trails on Luke's belly as he moved. His orgasm built, sending tingles the length of his spine and when it came there was no stopping. With a final deep, powerful thrust into Skye's welcoming heat, Luke came with an exultant shout. Beneath him Skye bucked, his body rippling, his muscles pulling Luke deeper. He cried out as he came, tears rolling down his face. Luke collapsed onto him, holding him tight, kissing him over and over again. It was a while until he realized that he must be crushing Skye with his weight. He shifted onto his back, pulling Skye on top of him, not wanting even inches to separate them.

"I love you, Skye." He murmured the words into Skye's hair knowing that they came from deep within him rather than from the heat of the moment.

"That's good, Sir because I love you too." Skye snuggled against him, giving his chest flickering licks of his tongue and sweet kisses. "Thank you for making this so perfect."

"I didn't hurt you?"

"How long till we can do it again?"

Skye's response made Luke laugh. "As soon as you like, so long as you're not sore and you give me a while to recover. I'm not as young as you. Would you like to take a shower?"

"Only if you want to, Sir. We're just going to get all sticky again and I like it right here." He held on tighter.

Luke stroked his back and his butt, memorizing the curves and dimples. "You know, I can't wait to fuck you on the St. Andrew's cross, over the spanking bench, while you're chained and gagged and have no choice but to take me however I choose."

Skye moaned. "You're making me hard, Sir. You will let me come every now and again, won't you?"

"If you're good." Luke pressed a finger into Skye's arse. He yelped, then wiggled trying to encourage Luke deeper. "I think you're forgetting who's in charge here, love." Luke withdrew his finger before giving Skye's backside several sharp spanks.

"Sorry, Sir." Skye didn't sound remorseful at all. He sounded joyful. Luke smiled. It would be fun to think up some inventive punishments for his naughty sub, but for now he was happy just to hold him. Skye was where he was meant to be, safe, cherished and all Luke's.

It was an hour or so later when Luke awoke from a light doze to the sound of urgent knocking at his door.

"What now?" He extracted himself from beneath Skye's body, grabbed his robe and went to see who it was disturbing his peace. To his surprise, he found

Rayne in the corridor hopping from foot to foot in agitation.

"I'm so sorry to disturb you, Mr. Redding, but you need to come down to the kitchen. There's something you have to see." Rayne was stressed, his worry genuine.

"Can you give me a few minutes?" Luke asked. He smelled of sex and sweat. Getting clean was a priority.

Rayne nodded before jogging down the corridor. "Please be quick, sir."

Skye had woken and was sitting up in bed with a bewildered expression on his face. "What's happening, Sir? Was that Rayne?"

"I don't know what's going on, but I need to go down to the kitchen. I'm going to take a quick shower. I'm sure Rayne would have said if the situation was life or death."

Skye scrambled out of bed. "I'll come with you."

Showering together without it turning into something more took a significant effort of will. Luke pulled on his discarded clothes, not bothering to search out anything clean. Looking anxious, Skye dressed just as quickly.

Skye grabbed his hand as they ran down the stairs and through to the kitchen. They found Rayne, Benjy, Frank, Fergus and Henry gathered around the table in the staff room. A large cardboard box sat in the middle of it and there were strange squeaks coming from inside.

"Will someone tell me what's going on?" Luke demanded

Skye peered into the box. "Oh! Oh, look, Sir."

Frustrated that no one was giving him a clear explanation for the chaos, Luke stepped forward. For a moment he couldn't work out what he was looking at, but gradually he realized that the pile of wriggling fur in the box was a collection of kittens and their mother, an ample tabby with a purr like a traction engine.

"Perhaps someone could explain why there is a box of cats on the table?"

Skye pulled one of the kittens from the box and held it against his chest where it promptly fell asleep. "Where did they come from?" he asked.

"They were left outside the main gate," Rayne said. "I drove into the village because I had to get my mum's birthday card into the post and when I got back the box was there. Right in the middle of the road. How could somebody just dump them?"

By this time, all the boys had picked out a kitten to cuddle. The mother cat didn't seem bothered at all. *Probably relieved to get a moment's peace,* Luke thought. *I know how she feels.*

Skye turned to Luke with pleading eyes. "Can we keep them, Sir?"

Luke found himself the subject of six intense stares. He had the sense to recognize he'd already lost the battle. Thoughts of the sub mafia flashed through his head. "They can stay for the weekend, then we will have to see about finding them new homes. They also need to visit a vet. They can't be anywhere near the kitchen though. Tor would have me hung like an aging ham." He surveyed his staff. "You'll all have to take turns looking after them, and that includes the night shift. I suggest the old chauffeur's room over the garage would be suitable. It's well insulated and dry."

"We can set up a pen so they have some space to play," Benjy suggested. "And find something cozy for them to sleep in."

"They'll need food, a litter tray... I grew up with cats," Henry said. "If you drive, Rayne, we could get to the nearest pet superstore. The place will be open until eight tonight and there's a vet on site. I'll call them and see if we can get an emergency appointment."

"The kittens aren't weaned yet," Rayne said. "They've been feeding from their mum, so we won't need kitten food. I think someone else should come with us. I don't want any of them getting loose in the car and we don't have a proper pet carrier.

Luke listened as the planning continued around him. With the decision made that the cats could stay, he had become superfluous to the proceedings. "Frank, for those who are staying in tonight, please order a takeaway from the Happy Garden. You can use The Retreat's account. I'll leave you all to it. I have a date with a glass of wine and a few episodes of *Luther* on the iPlayer. I'll be in my quarters if you need me." He directed the last comment to Skye who seemed torn between joining him and staying to play with the kittens. He gave the one he was holding a kiss before putting it back in the box.

"Include me in the cat-sitting rota," Skye said. "That's okay, isn't it, Sir?"

"It is." He was pleased Skye had volunteered. "They'll be back from the vet's soon enough," he said, taking Skye's hand and leading him from the staff room. "In the meantime, you can pet me instead."

Skye licked his lips. "Yes please, Sir!"

Luke guessed he retained around ninety-nine percent of Skye's love. The other percent had gone to a box of wriggling fluff balls.

Chapter Sixteen

Once they were back in his room, Luke poured himself a glass of wine then drank a big gulp before topping it up again. "Rayne needs to learn how not to give someone a heart attack. I thought there had been an accident, or that may be the place was burning down, when he banged at the door. The last thing I expected was a collection of furry house guests. Would you like a glass?"

"No, thank you Sir. I don't like the taste and I have no capacity for alcohol. One small glass of my grandmother's sherry at Christmas and I turn into a giggling mess that won't stop talking. I'll just have a glass of water. It's safer. Can you believe how cute the kittens were?"

"There's a bottle of Perrier in the fridge, if you'd like that?"

"Ooh, bubbles! Yes, please."

Luke unscrewed the bottle, releasing a fizz. He poured some into a tumbler then handed it to Skye. "They were cute, I admit it. Here you go. Is there anything you'd prefer to watch on TV? I can save my *Luther* bingeing for another time."

"I'm quite happy to sit and watch Idris Elba any time, Sir." Skye sipped his water and concentrated on the bubbles bursting on his tongue rather than Luke's reaction to that statement, which had just slipped out.

"Well that makes two of us, so you're forgiven for lusting after him. This time."

Luke kicked off his shoes then took a seat at one end of the sofa, bringing his legs up to rest along its length. He patted the space between them. "I think we'll both have a good view from here."

Skye settled into place, his back resting against Luke's chest. He gave a contented sigh. "I think this is my second favorite place to be," he said.

"What's the first?" Luke asked.

"In bed with you, Sir." Skye's cheeks heated. Luke wrapped both arms around him and he snuggled into his hold. "It was kind of you to let the cats stay, Sir. I don't understand how anyone could dump them like that."

"If I'd said no, I would have been afraid for my life. They seemed healthy enough," Luke said, ruffling his hair. "Perhaps whoever abandoned them knew that they'd be seen and picked up quickly. You understand we can't keep them here long-term though, cute as they are?"

"Could you think about letting us have one or two?" Skye asked, wondering at his own bravery. "They'd earn their keep making sure we never get a mice problem, wouldn't they?"

"You have a soft heart. We'll see. Animals are a big responsibility and we can't have them in the main house in case any of our guests have allergies, but I promise to think about it."

"I understand, Sir." Secretly, Skye thought Luke had just as soft a heart as he did. The cat and her kittens would have a home until something better could be found for them. They'd be well fed and get lots of love. That was all Skye could hope for. He jerked, nearly spilling his water, when Luke slipped a hand between his shirt buttons to tweak a nipple. He didn't say anything. In fact, his attention seemed to be entirely on the television, but every now and again he rolled Skye's sensitive nub between his fingers or gave it a gentle pinch. Skye's cock sprang to life and he wiggled in an attempt to get more comfortable. He missed the chastity device, which Luke had left off after they'd made love.

Luke slid his other hand from Skye's waist to his groin, covering the bulge of his erection. Skye gave a strangled moan. If Luke moved his hand then Skye was going to come, no doubt about it.

"Sir..."

"Watch the program, Skye."

Skye twisted around to see Luke's expression, but he seemed to have his attention fixed to the screen. Despite this, he managed to move both his hands at once, squeezing Skye's dick at the same time as pinching a nipple. Skye yelped and came, gasping for breath. Luke was still watching the program, seemingly unmoved by his plight. After a few moments of deep breathing, Skye recovered enough to speak.

"Um, I need to use the bathroom, Sir. I think I should take a quick shower." Coming in his clothes was not a comfortable experience.

"Go ahead." Luke released his hold. He unbuckled Skye's collar. "Don't bother putting any clothes back on."

Realizing that he had been well and truly played, Skye waddled to the en suite, stripped off his clothes and took a very quick shower. He toweled dry then, with some regret, dumped the damp towel and his sticky clothes in the laundry basket. As he walked, naked, back toward the sofa he caught Luke's grin even though he tried to hide it.

Skye dropped to his knees. "I'm sorry I came without permission, Sir."

"I'm not. It gives me an excuse to punish you."

"I didn't think you needed an excuse, Sir."

Luke chuckled. "True and I'm glad you recognize that." He stroked Skye's neck as he fastened his collar. "But that can wait until later. Come sit with me."

Skye resumed his previous position. Luke arranged him so that Skye's legs rested over Luke's, spreading him wide. He pulled a throw from the back of the sofa and laid it over them. Skye's momentary relief that he was covered disappeared when Luke pushed a hand beneath the throw to fondle Skye's cock.

"Mmm, you make a fine hand warmer."

"I think you're very wicked, Sir." Skye's dick made a valiant attempt to rise.

"I'm afraid so."

Luke's hand wasn't nearly as effective as a chastity cage. That Skye hardened beneath his touch was as inevitable as the next day's sunrise. He couldn't focus on the program so drifted into the self-preservation of his thoughts. From nowhere he wondered what his father would think if he could see him now. He'd be proud. Not that Skye sat with another man's hand gripping his privates, but that he had found someone to be with who he could love and trust. He wouldn't have cared that Luke was a Dominant, that he was older or that he felt the need to spank Skye's backside on regular occasions. He would have accepted Skye's choice and welcomed Luke into the family. The burn of shame heated Skye's cheek. It was long past time to share his history.

"Sir, I want to tell you about what happened to my dad. Why my hair changed color."

Luke stilled. He pressed the remote, turning off the television. He didn't try to change Skye's mind, nor did he move his hand. Skye took it as the act of possession it was.

"Meeting Professor Doring had a strange irony to it, Sir. My dad was a keen diver. He always had been, and as soon as I was old enough he made sure I got my PADI training. I don't remember my mum—I wasn't even one year old when she died. I think I told you, she had a hereditary condition that made her susceptible to infection because of a weak immune system. She contracted pneumonia after a spell of bronchitis and wasn't strong enough to fight it. There were photos, of course, and Dad was willing to talk about her, but I tended not to ask because it made him sad."

"Are you in danger from this condition?" Luke held Skye tighter.

"No. I was tested young. It skipped a generation with me. Apparently it's much less common in boys than girls."

"That's a relief. I want you whole and healthy for as long as possible."

"After Mum died, we moved in with my dad's parents so Grandma could help take care of me. Dad made my childhood as much fun as he could and diving was a big part of it. Most weekends we'd drive to the south coast to explore the wrecks around Fort Bovisand. I loved it. Underwater, it felt like the whole world belonged to us. I never got tired of watching the fish. No matter how early I had to haul myself out of bed, it was always worthwhile. In the holidays he even took me to places in Greece and Italy where the diving was particularly good. Once we went to the East coast of Egypt's Sinai Peninsula to one of the world's most beautiful diving spots, the Blue Hole. It's this amazing coral-lined, three-hundred-and-ninety-four-foot deep sink hole. I'll always remember that trip. I have pictures I can show you."

"I'd like that very much."

"Dad was always careful, meticulous, about safety and preparation, but in the end, it didn't help him." Skye took a deep breath. It was the first time he had talked about this since it had happened. For years he had built a thick, armored shell around his emotions, but Luke had been breaking through that since the moment they'd met. "It was a beautiful autumn day, and we were up before dawn to get to a spot on the north Cornish coast. In his diving circles, Dad had heard a rumor of a new discovery—a man-'o-war blown off course by a storm sometime in the eighteenth century. Because the wreck was so deep, we picked up extra oxygen tanks from a supplier onshore then took a boat about half a mile or so out to sea. Dad had calculated the time we would need to resurface because we had to do it in stages to avoid getting the bends. We found the wreck on just the second attempt and it was amazing, though partly covered by shifting sand. The cannon could be seen, all barnacle-encrusted, and the anchor."

He was avoiding the crux of the story. "There was a problem with one of Dad's tanks. He had gone through the oxygen supply much quicker than he should have. We could have shared my oxygen — it wasn't enough to avoid both of us getting the bends, but there would have been a higher chance of survival. He didn't tell me. We were tied together and he let himself die to save me. He breathed poison — for me. Nitrogen built in his blood and he had a fatal embolism. His body was connected to mine for three hours while I made my way to the surface." Hot tears rolled down Skye's cheeks. "My hair turned silver over the following months. The doctors said it was a rare form of alopecia exacerbated by stress from the shock. It's a myth that hair can change color overnight. I was in a bad place for a long time." He turned in Luke's arms, needing his comfort as the horrific events of that day crashed back into his head.

For a while Luke said nothing, just soothed him with gentle touches.

"Your father was a selfless, brave man and I wish I could have met him." He pulled the throw around Skye's shoulders. "You made some wonderful memories with him and that's what you should remember. After his sacrifice, you owe it to him to be happy."

"You sound like my grandparents," Skye said, snuffling against Luke's shirt, soaking the thin cotton with his tears. "After the accident, the farm was never the same place for me. I went away to university and never went back."

"Your home is here now, with me. I would like to meet you grandparents one day, when you feel ready."

"Grandpa will love you. He's strong like you are. Grandma will live up to grandmother stereotypes everywhere and want to feed you. She makes the most amazing cakes and cookies. She could teach Tor a thing or two."

"I understand now why you said you don't swim."

"I haven't been in the water since it happened. It's a stupid phobia, I know."

"Not stupid at all. With the pool here, if you ever want to just dangle your feet over the edge, let me know and I'll hold your hand. You'd get to see me in swimming trunks if nothing else."

Luke's dry tone and injection of humor made Skye smile. "Thank you, Sir. Since I met you, I've been able to think about Dad without dissolving into an emotional mess. I know it wasn't my fault and I understand why he made the decision he did, but it's hard to be grateful when he's gone."

"He wouldn't want your gratitude just that you live your life to the fullest."

"Well, in that case, Sir…" Skye scrubbed his eyes with the back of his hand. "Don't you think we should take advantage of being alone together?"

Luke swiveled around and stood in one fluid movement, holding Skye in his arms. The throw fell away, leaving him bare. Luke deposited him on the bed then proceeded to take off his clothes, Skye watching with undisguised delight. Luke plumped his pillows before sitting on the bed next to Skye.

"I think you should do all the work this time. Grab the lube and prepare yourself for me. Turn around, so I can see what you're doing."

Skye coated two fingers with lube. He knelt across Luke's legs facing away from him then pushed the slick digits into his channel, grunting at the slight pinch of penetration. Skye's face burned as he pictured Luke's view.

"Very pretty," Luke said. "I think that's enough. Turn around."

Skye managed to relocate so that he was facing Luke without kicking or kneeing him. He shuffled forward so that his arse was over Luke's erection.

"Go at your own pace. You don't have my permission to come and this time, there will be consequences if you do."

In small increments, Skye lowered himself onto Luke's cock. There was an initial ache but nothing he couldn't manage. He felt so full. The position seemed to drive Luke deep into his body.

"That's it. Now raise and lower yourself."

"Yes, Sir." Smooth movements proved to be impossible. Skye's leg muscles wouldn't cooperate. They twitched, making him jerk every time he moved. Luke raised his knees, penetrating him even farther. He grabbed Skye's hips and took control, lifting and dropping him. Skye reached for his cock, desperate to come, but Luke knocked his hand away.

"Don't you dare!"

Skye focused on bringing Luke to his climax. He squeezed with his inner muscles, rippling his body as Luke manhandled him.

"Holy fuck!" Luke yelled and heat filled Skye's channel as Luke came. Luke dug his fingers into Skye's hips and the pain brought Skye even closer to the edge. He rode Luke's orgasm, pleading with his eyes as best he knew how. With a wicked smirk, Luke flicked the end of Skye's cock.

"Come!"

The added flash of pain sent lightning to Skye's balls. He screamed Luke's name, his orgasm rolling through him and his entire body racked with shivers. Luke pulled him down into a hug, wrapping him in warmth.

"It's all right, sweetheart. Just let it go. You're safe with me and you always will be."

Skye sobbed, his tangled emotions a confusion of joy and sadness. Still joined to Luke, he felt like he never wanted to move again.

Baring his soul had been exhausting but somehow liberating. He had not been comfortable holding something so important back from Luke. He wanted his Dom to know him inside out and his history was a part of that. He dozed against Luke's body, relishing every gentle touch and murmured word of comfort.

Waking felt like emerging from the cocoon, exciting and full of opportunity but at the same time a little terrifying.

"You know, the boys will be disappointed if we don't join them for the Chinese feast," Luke said. "But if you'd rather stay here…"

Skye rubbed his eyes. "No, I'd love to join them if you don't mind, Sir. I don't, I mean, would you not tell them any of this? They don't need to know. I don't want them looking at me differently, if you see what I mean?"

"It's between you and me," Luke said. "I would never share anything so personal without your permission."

"It's history. It's a part of me, but I can't let it rule my life. That's your job now, Sir." He gave Luke a sideways glance, hoping that Luke recognized the humor in his statement. Luke rolled him over and gave his arse a couple of hard spanks.

"Well I certainly rule this, and I think it needs to be nice and pink for the rest of the evening." Several more smacks had Skye squirming to escape. "You need another shower, brat. Now."

Getting clean became a whole new adventure when sharing a shower with Luke. Skye's knees ached by the time he had sucked Luke to the edge of orgasm. Then he gave thanks for waterproof lube as Luke pushed him against the tile and fucked him until he screamed.

Having his collar put back on seemed almost ceremonial, but Skye loved the look of satisfaction on Luke's face as he tightened the buckle and checked the fit. He replaced the cock cage with gentle, deft movements then had Skye bend over the bed while he inserted a small plug. "Can't have you feeling empty this evening." He patted Skye's backside eliciting a yelp. "You can get dressed now."

"Thank you, Sir," Skye said with a measure of sarcasm. He wished he could wear something softer than jeans while his backside recovered from the spanking, but despite the slight pain, he felt contented. Luke's touch was on his cock, in his arse, on his skin. He needed it as much as he needed air.

Downstairs, the staff room was full of Chinese takeaway boxes and a vast array of cat paraphernalia. Skye was astonished to find the kittens sound asleep in their box while their mother, curled on one of the chairs, took a leisurely wash. Considering the racket going on all around them, he was amazed they could get any rest at all.

With a resigned sigh, Luke accepted the cup of tea he was handed then settled into the chair at the end of the table. Someone—Skye guessed it had been Rayne—handed Luke the newspaper, which he promptly unfolded and hid behind.

Skye sat with care, catching Rayne's knowing glance as he did so. He frowned, trying to warn Rayne not to say anything embarrassing.

"You're looking a little...uncomfortable, Skye. Would you like a cushion?"

Skye should have known that he could not rely on Rayne's discretion. He sighed. "How are the kittens, Rayne?" he said through gritted teeth.

"The vet was a sweetheart. She checked them all over and gave them a clean bill of health. They have to go back for some jabs when they're a bit older. They don't have fleas, thank the Lord, and she gave us a whole load of leaflets about kitten care and told us what we needed to buy to look after them properly."

"We thought you could help us with an advertising campaign to find them good new homes," Benjy said. "You're good at computer stuff. You found all those quotes and things for the *Brideshead* dinner."

"I'd love to," Skye said. "It's really important that they go to places where they'll get lots of love." He caught Luke's eye and gave him his most appealing look. Luke shook his head and went back to his paper. Luke's defenses wouldn't be too difficult to break through. He was determined that The Retreat should have its own cat. Or two. He knew he'd have the support of all the subs and between them it wouldn't be a problem to look after two small animals, even if they weren't allowed in the main house. The Retreat's grounds were cat heaven. It was fate that the furry family had been delivered to its gates and Skye was hopeful that he could persuade Luke to let one or two stay.

As he munched on his Chinese food, Skye couldn't help but daydream about how lucky he was. He had an amazing Dom, an exciting new job doing the research he loved, and now the potential for furry friends. It was hard to imagine how life could get any better.

Chapter Seventeen

Over the following weeks, Skye found that he loved his hectic but satisfying life. Luke took his training seriously and spent time every day working with him on things as simple as being able to kneel with grace, to more challenging tests of his control where, forbidden to come, Luke would edge him for what seemed like hours. Luke tested his boundaries, using a range of toys and equipment. The exploration, the newness of it all was exciting and Skye discovered he enjoyed a certain level of pain, but not beyond. Luke's sadism veered more toward denial than pain, which suited them both. They were made for each other, their kinks compatible, their needs complementary.

Luke had replaced Skye's leather collar with one fashioned from etched stainless steel. It had Luke's name engraved on the inside and never came off. It gave Skye the sense of security he craved and he touched it all the time, affirming his status as belonging to Luke.

Sue Doring proved to be a flexible if somewhat demanding boss. Skye thought she'd make a good Domme if she ever felt inclined. She accepted his relationship with Luke without question, including him in all decisions about Skye's work and the time he needed to spend on it. As time went by and Skye proved his ability, she gave him more complex tasks that exercised his brain and piqued his curiosity. He had even written an article about his research, which the professor had endorsed and submitted to an academic periodical. When it was published, Luke threw a staff party at The Retreat and the professor came along, exclaiming at the originality of the house and hugging all the boys. She had promised to visit every time she was in the country, just to taste more of Tor's cooking.

Skye's social media campaign for the kittens had found homes for five of the six. Having Fergus and Henry pose shirtless with the kittens in their arms had proved a big draw when Alistair sent the pictures out to The Underground's entire membership list. The mother cat, now named Lucky, ruled over her new empire from cozy accommodations above the garage, bossing her remaining daughter, Marshmallow, during their daily mouse hunts. It was a regular occurrence that one or the other of them would sneak into the main house and have to be ejected, though some of the guests were guilty of enticing them inside. The fire in the banqueting hall proved irresistible to felines. Claw marks in leather were the biggest problems as the toughest Doms succumbed to furry appeals for a comfortable lap.

Guests came and went, some becoming friends as Skye's shyness receded and his confidence grew. He now looked forward to the new arrivals and, despite his burgeoning academic career, still loved serving at mealtimes, especially since Luke had put a ban on him wearing costumes that were too skimpy.

Breaks between the guests were treasured and it was during one of these that Skye persuaded Frank to teach him how to bake cookies.

"Luke loves a cookie with his morning coffee," Skye said, standing in the kitchen wearing an apron over his clothes. "I don't want to get in the way, but it would be nice for me to be able to tell him that I baked some of them myself."

"And so you shall." Frank grinned. "I'm going to show you how to make the chocolate ginger ones because there's not much Luke won't do to get his hands on them. You should make them when you've been naughty, because he'll forgive you anything if you produce a plate of them."

Skye doubted that Luke could be bribed by something as simple as a cookie. Besides, he tried to be good. Submission came naturally to him. It wasn't something he rebelled against, but every now and again he forgot the time when he was buried in his research or neglected to eat when he was busy serving guests and those were punishable offenses. Luke was strict about him looking after himself and inventive when it came to punishment.

"The secret to these is the amount of crystallized ginger. That's what gives them their intense flavor," Frank explained. "So, first of all you need to cream together the butter and the two different kinds of sugar. Then you get to beat in the vanilla and the egg, which is so therapeutic, especially when Tor's in a bad mood."

Snickering, Skye weighed out the ingredients then put some welly into beating everything together until it looked creamy.

"Next, we melt the chocolate in the microwave until it's smooth and runny. I always make sure there's a bit of extra chocolate to nibble, just to make sure it tastes right, you know?"

Skye broke up the bar of intensely dark chocolate, sharing the leftover pieces with Frank while it melted. Then he got to stir it into the mixture, changing it from cream to a deep brown color.

"Okay, now you need to stir in the crystallized ginger. I used to use the raw roots, but the guests are always requesting it, so I gave up and use this type now."

"That stuff stings." Skye's arse clenched at the memory of the last time Luke had experimented with a piece of raw ginger. "Why's it called figging anyway? Figs are a whole different thing."

Frank laughed. "I wouldn't know, or how it feels. One day." He sounded a bit wistful.

"You'll find someone," Skye said. "I hope you're as lucky as I am."

"Luke's one of a kind," Frank said. "I think I'd need someone a bit more lenient. I'll be heading back to The Underground soon, which will give me a chance to go Dom shopping." He checked Skye's mixture. "Now you've added the chopped ginger, you need to mix together the flour, bicarbonate of soda and a pinch of salt then we combine them with the other ingredients until they're well mixed."

"How long will they take to cook?" Skye asked as he stirred.

"Only ten minutes or so. I like this recipe because it's not the kind of dough you have to chill in the fridge. As long as we space the dollops out on the baking tray, they shouldn't spread into each other."

Skye spooned even portions of his mixture onto the baking trays Frank had prepared for him then slid them into the oven.

"Now we have time for a cuppa, while they bake. We have to let them sit for a couple of minutes on the tray when we take them out, and after that it's a free for all."

"Yummy." Skye had managed to get flour and cookie mixture over most of his body. He wasn't sure how. He helped Frank clear up then they sat chatting over a cup of tea while the kitchen filled with a wonderful aroma of baking cookies. The scent drew Fergus and Henry to the kitchen and it wasn't long before Rayne joined them. They all sat with expectant looks on their faces.

"You know I'm baking these for Luke, right?" Skye said, exasperated.

"Luke is going to have to share," Rayne said.

"Share what?" Luke appeared in the doorway.

"I'm baking you cookies as a surprise, Sir, but the vultures have already descended. It's a good job we don't have any guests in today or they would be in here too, no doubt."

"I was wondering what you'd been getting up to. I have plans for you and me in the dungeon, but a coffee break will set me up for the exercise quite well, I think."

There were snickers from around the table.

"You're blushing, love. I thought you were beyond that." Luke took a seat at the table.

"Sir..." Skye protested, his complaint cut off by the sound of the timer going off in the kitchen. "Oh, they're done!" He and Frank rushed into the kitchen where Skye had the honor of withdrawing the baking trays from the oven.

"They're perfect." Skye admired the misshapen results of his first baking efforts. "And they smell so good."

"You'd better make sure you eat a few," Frank said. "If Luke's taking you to the dungeon for the rest of the day, you'll need the sugar."

Skye levered the cookies onto a wire cooling rack, which he carried through to the staff room and placed in the center of the table. Frank delivered some plates, which he laid in front of everyone before pouring more tea.

"You're supposed to wait for them to cool," Skye said, as several people grabbed the still-hot cookies.

"Too good to wait," Rayne muttered, his mouth full.

Skye gave up. He presented Luke with two cookies and waited for his verdict.

"These are delicious," Luke said. "Just as good as the ones Frank and Benjy bake."

Skye knew it wasn't true, but he loved Luke for saying it anyway. He hoped he had earned himself at least one orgasm with his efforts. He'd bake every day if that was the case. He fidgeted in his seat, wondering what Luke had planned. He had proved to be creative during their previous visits to the dungeon and the anticipation set Skye's nerves tingling.

"I'll meet you downstairs in half an hour," Luke said as he pushed his chair back and stood. "You won't need the apron, and you might consider hosing off some of that flour."

After thanking Frank for his help, Skye scuttled upstairs to prepare himself. A quick shower followed his daily tussle with the enema kit. For once he wore no chastity device or plug, but he guessed that state wouldn't last long if Luke had anything to do with it.

The man had a penchant for keeping him locked up and stuffed full. He didn't object.

Knowing that he would have to strip as soon as he got to the dungeon, Skye slipped into a pair of old jeans and a T-shirt. He didn't bother with shoes, socks or underwear. Remaining clothed while Skye was naked was one of Luke's biggest kinks and in Luke's opinion Skye's underwear was only ever fit to be torn off.

It was quiet in the dungeon. Skye took off his clothes then picked a spot in the middle of the central room. He knelt in the position Luke preferred, with his hands behind his back and thighs spread. Already excited, his cock bobbed, the gleam of pre-cum highlighting its tip. Skye fixed his eyes on the floor and waited. It wasn't long before he heard the tread of heavy boots on the stone steps. Glancing up from beneath his lashes, he gasped. Luke wore skin-tight leather trousers that rode low on his hips. His boots had thick soles and buckles at the sides and his black shirt was unbuttoned, the gauzy fabric lifting in the slight breeze generated by the space heaters. The icing on this lust-inducing cake was the spectacles balanced on Luke's aquiline nose and the leather gloves on his hands. Skye's cock jerked and the temptation to reach for it almost overwhelmed him. He resisted because he knew Luke would be disappointed if he gave in to the urge.

"You may stand." Luke took up a position in front of Skye. "Spread your legs, bend over and grab your ankles."

Skye held the well-practiced position with ease while Luke walked around him. The first time Luke had examined him this way, Skye's face had burned from the humiliation but now he realized it was just Luke's unique method of checking that he wasn't too sore to play. Luke pulled his arse cheeks apart then fingered Skye's hole.

"Good. Remain as you are while I make some preparations."

If he tried to get a look at what Luke was doing, Skye would lose his balance. He was forced to contain his curiosity and stay still. The noises Luke made gave nothing away.

"Okay, straighten up. I don't think you've seen the new cross yet, have you? It was only delivered this week. I had it moved down here so we could try it out."

Skye examined the X-shaped cross that now stood on a platform in the center of the room. It was different from the other St Andrew's cross in the dungeon in that it had a frame and a crossbar that dissected the center of the X. Cuffs were affixed at the end of each section, and at the bottom these were above two small shelves.

"Present your back to the cross. Stand on the steps."

Still wondering what he was missing, Skye got into position. On the steps, he was a good three feet above the floor and Luke had to use a stool to fasten the Velcro straps around his wrists. A wide belt went around his waist, and two more straps around his ankles.

"Now for the surprise. It's quite secure, I promise, but you have your safe word if you need it." Luke released a mechanism at the side of the frame, cranked a handle and Skye yelped as the cross inverted inside the frame, suspending him upside down. His head was now three feet above the ground, at the perfect height for Luke's cock. Skye's gaze darted here and there, tinged with panic as he tried to get his bearings, until Luke unbuttoned his fly. He pressed the head of his cock to Skye's lips. "Focus on me, sweetheart."

Suckling Luke's erection had a settling familiarity. Skye stopped struggling and settled on his task, licking and sucking happily. When Luke pulled away, Skye was much calmer. Hanging upside down was strange, but if that was where Luke wanted him, that was where he was content to be.

Luke took a soft suede flogger from a hook on the wall, letting the strands run through his fingers. He walked behind the cross and a slight hiss was the only warning Skye got before he struck for the first time. Luke laid stroke after stroke across Skye's thighs and buttocks, not hitting him hard but enough to build heat beneath his skin. Every now and again a strand would curl between his legs, catching his balls. Skye flexed his fingers then curled them into fists, absorbing the pain. He was on the verge of using his safe word when Luke stopped, then rotated the cross back to the upright position. For a moment Skye felt a little dizzy, but the sensation soon faded. When Luke released him from the cross, he was steady enough to make it to the spanking bench under his own steam. He was still hard and his balls tingled from the flogging. Luke had him stand at the end of the bench, resting his chest and belly on its flat surface. He then bound Skye's hands to handles on the side of the equipment.

"Spread your legs wider."

The only way Skye could achieve this was to go onto his tiptoes. His inner thigh muscles protested at the stretch. The tip of his cock brushed the end of the bench.

"You can come, but not before I do," Luke said. "I can promise you won't enjoy your punishment if you do."

Skye whimpered then gasped as Luke pushed deep inside him. The cold lube coating Luke's cock soon warmed as he drove into Skye's channel over and over again, gripping Skye's hips to steady himself.

"Don't come, don't come, don't come." Skye repeated the mantra. It crossed his mind that instead he should be begging Luke to come so that he could follow. He laughed, a little hysterical, but then Luke gave one final, powerful thrust and the liquid heat of his release filled Skye's passage. Less than a second later, he let himself go, yelling as Luke wrapped a hand around his cock, jerking him until he ran dry.

Skye's vision swam, his mind and body overwhelmed by sensation. Luke steadied him with a hand on his arse while he released Skye's hands.

"Keep still. I'm going to plug my seed inside you." Luke's voice was as rough as gravel but his hands gentle as he inserted a thick plug. "Okay, you can stand. How are you feeling?"

Skye's answer was to fall into Luke's hold, letting his Dominant support his weight because his legs were no longer capable. Luke scooped him into his arms then carried him to the low, rubber-sheeted bed at one side of the dungeon. "We'll take a few minutes to recover here then we'll go upstairs where I can pamper you properly. I have some new balm that will cool your back."

"Sounds perfect, Sir." Skye cuddled against Luke's body. "You look hot in leather. You should wear it more often." He snuffled, his eyes drooping. "I think you broke me, Sir."

"And you enjoyed every second."

"I wasn't sure about the whole upside-down thingy at first," Skye confessed. "But I think the guests will love it."

"Well, I wanted to do something special. It's the last chance we will have to play down here for quite a while with all the bookings we have coming up." He stroked Skye's back. "Thank you for trusting me."

Skye sighed, contented and warm in Luke's arms. He was just where he wanted to be. "Always, Sir."

* * * *

Recipe for Chocolate Ginger Cookies, from allrecipes.co.uk

Ingredients
Makes: 15 biscuits
115g unsalted butter
50g caster sugar
70g light brown soft sugar
1/2 teaspoon vanilla extract
1 large egg
70g 70% cacao dark chocolate
65g finely chopped crystallised ginger
160g plain flour
1/4 teaspoon bicarbonate of soda
1 pinch salt

Method
Prep: 20min › Cook: 10min › Extra time: 2min cooling › Ready in: 32min
Preheat the oven to 180 C / Gas 4. Grease 2 baking trays.
Cream together butter and sugars until combined. Beat in the vanilla and the egg.

Melt the chocolate in the microwave gently until smooth and runny and stir into the mixture, then add the chopped ginger.

Mix together flour, bicarb and a pinch of salt and combine with the other ingredients until just mixed. Place heaped tablespoons onto baking tray, well-spaced.

Bake in oven for 9 to 11 minutes. Let sit for a couple of minutes on tray and move to a wire cooling rack.

Devour!

Want to see more from L.M. Somerton? Here's a taster for you to enjoy!

Fairground Attractions: Ghost Train
L.M. Somerton

Excerpt

"Four teas, my lovelies. Food'll be out in a minute." Mo, proprietor of the eponymous Mo's Café, deposited her tray on the edge of the table before setting a steaming mug in front of each of her four customers. "You boys back for the summer then?"

"Why else would we be here taking in the delights of your homage to seventies décor, Mo?" Garth accompanied his words with a sweep of his hand, displaying black-painted nails. He got a clip around the ear for his trouble.

"Cheeky boy." Mo grinned. "It's good to see you. You all look the same—except you, sweetie." She ruffled Stevie's candy-floss hair. "This was blue last year, but the lilac suits you."

Stevie blushed to the roots of his mop and started to play with the salt cellar. Zach squeezed his shoulder.

"It'll go well with the products on your stall, Stevie."

Stevie gazed at him, his silver-gray eyes huge. "I'm not working at the candy-floss concession this year, Zach. I'm going to be running the carousel." He sounded proud.

"Wow! That's quite a promotion. The carousel's a prime spot and so much fun. Dad's put me back on the helter-skelter, which I think is his way of telling me I need more exercise, and Garth is on the ghost train as usual."

Garth grinned. "Where else would he put me?" He flicked an imaginary piece of lint from the shoulder of his black leather jacket. "I fit right in."

"What is it they call all that black?" Mo asked. "Gouda, gaudy... No, neither of those sounds right. Ghastly?"

"He's a Goth, Mo," Zach explained, raising his voice to be heard above his friends' laughter. Mo wandered back to the counter, muttering about weird fashion sense and clothing better suited to funerals.

Garth shrugged. "She loves me." He extracted a black lipstick from his jacket pocket then applied a fresh coat. "Last year she asked me if I'd been an extra in *Interview with The Vampire*. That film came out in 1994. I wasn't even born!" He sniffed and examined his fingernails. "What about you, Adam? What's Zach's dad got you doing this year?"

Adam pushed his shoulders back and stuck his chest out. "Security. Same as before. He said I have to keep you three in line." He raised his mug of tea in a toast. "Though he also admitted it was a hopeless task."

Garth gave his friend the once over, admiring his well-muscled physique. Adam looked exactly like the county and England rugby player he was. He was a head taller than the rest of them at six foot four. Garth only made six feet because of his thick-soled biker boots. Stevie, the smallest of the group, had topped out at five foot six and Zach only a couple of inches more. Stand them in a line and they made a great slope.

"You have more chance of convincing Mo not to serve black pudding with her full English. Never gonna happen." Zach clinked his mug against Adam's. "But have at it. Stevie at least will enjoy you telling him what to do."

Adam's half-laugh told them that he would enjoy that just as much. Stevie's pale cheeks pinked.

"Don't tease me," he muttered, not making eye contact. "You're no different."

Garth had the chance to contemplate Stevie's words as Mo arrived to deposit four heaped plates in front of them. His arteries hardened as he examined the fragrant display of fried food. He inhaled the aroma before stabbing a sunshine-yellow egg yolk with his fork. "This summer, we're going to find the men of our dreams. Pride week will ensure there's plenty of choice. It's just a shame that blokes don't come labeled. It would save a lot of time and angsting if you could just check a tag that said *Dommy top, loves Shibari* or *Spankable sub seeks firm hand*. That kind of thing." He loaded his fork with bacon.

"So what would our tags say, genius?" Adam asked.

Garth raised a sculpted eyebrow. "I think Zach is the man to answer that one."

Apparently realizing he was under intense scrutiny from all three of his friends, Zach chewed, swallowed then took a swig of tea.

"Well, Stevie's easy. Sweet, shy size queen seeks extra-large Dom for pain-free pleasure."

Stevie shrugged. "He's good."

"What about me?" Garth asked.

"Emo brat pain slut, loves bondage, the stricter the better."

Scowling, Garth stuck his tongue out. Zach was spot on.

"He got you too, Garth," Stevie crowed. "Now it's Adam's turn."

Zach chewed on a piece of thick sausage, looking as if he were thinking it might provide suitable inspiration. "Over-protective Dom needs sub to take care of. Love of chastity essential."

Adam shoved a loaded fork into his mouth. He chewed and nodded in tandem. "Tag me now. I'm in."

"So what would your label say, Zach? Do you know yourself as well as you think you know us?" Garth asked. "It's one thing to describe your friends' kinks but entirely another to admit your own out loud."

"Zach only has eyes for one man," Stevie said. "A certain tall, dark professor in the maths department."

Garth and Adam murmured their agreement.

"Shame he's not interested," Zach said. "My tag will read *unrequited lust a specialty*."

"Professor Raynott *is* gorgeous," Stevie admitted. "But scary. I don't think I've ever seen him smile. Is he even gay?"

"He has a rainbow sticker in the back window of his Audi," Zach said. "I live in hope."

"Stalker!" Stevie waved a knife at him.

Zach shrugged. "My gaydar is non-existent. I wanted to know if I was barking up the wrong tree."

"More like an over-enthusiastic puppy peeing on the trunk." Adam snorted tea. Garth and Stevie fell about laughing.

"I'm glad you all find my love life, or lack of it, so amusing." Zach chuckled. "Even if I don't hook a duck with the hot professor's number on it, the summer promises to be entertaining."

"True," Garth agreed. It wasn't raining, Mo's breakfast was scrummy and he had two months to earn some cash and have fun with his friends. If any of them got lucky in the love lottery, they would celebrate together. "Life is good."

* * * *

Garth removed his leather jacket then placed it in the cubby reserved for his personal items. Ritual fashion humiliation came with the job. He could wear his own black trousers, but the royal blue polo shirt was compulsory. It had the amusement park's logo emblazoned across the back and Garth wouldn't have chosen to wear it if his life depended on it. He considered himself lucky to be working the ghost train. It was only two years old and state of the art — a much cooler place to work than the helter-skelter or the carousel. Zach would be run ragged, dragging coir mats around, and Stevie would be in a permanent state of giddiness.

The ghost train's special effects were terrifying and passengers expecting the kind of bone-shaking cheesy ride they might have experienced in their childhoods got the shock of their lives. Each carriage traveled through the ride on its own and, inside the cavernous warehouse that housed the experience, the layout was designed in a way that meant no carriage ever passed another. There was even a second story reached by a ramp, a tunnel and a section across a pool of inky water. An automatic camera took pictures of each car as it came through the exit doors. The expressions on customers' faces as they emerged into daylight were priceless.

The entire ride was run by a computer and a lot of complicated electronics. All Garth had to do was switch it on, recite safety instructions to the occupants of each car then press the button that sent them on their way. Customers could view their pictures on a big screen, but purchases were made via a central booth, so he didn't have to worry about taking money. It was mindless stuff, but he still had to be alert for any issues with the ride.

Every now and again, everything ground to a halt until he rebooted the computer. If that did happen, he had a Tannoy system to reassure anyone stuck inside. It wasn't difficult, the pay was okay and, best of all, he had plenty of time to give the occupants of the carriages a quick once-over in the hope of spotting Mr. Right. Of course, he hadn't the slightest idea what he might do if he did find Mr. Tall, Dark and Dominant, but he had plenty of time to daydream about the possibilities. It gave his brain a break from the intricacies of molecular physics and his skin a nice dose of vitamin D.

A bell sounded, signaling that the park had opened. The noise level built as rides whirred into action and pop music mixed in a clash of discordant harmonies. Soon the air would fill with the scent of hot dogs, toffee apples and deep-fried doughnuts all fighting for control of the visitors' olfactory senses. Garth focused on his building line of customers and got to work.

By the end of the day, his head was pounding. His back ached and his neck was so stiff he suspected a steel rod connected his skull to his spine. All he wanted to do was go home, soak in a hot bath for at least three hours, then crash. After a few days he'd get used to the work and the physical demands it placed on his body. Muscle memory didn't last a whole year and sitting in lecture theaters or the university library didn't prepare him for standing all day, bending over the cars on the ride. Home, however, was still a bike ride away.

Stevie always stayed with Zach over the holidays because his parents lived abroad, so he would catch a ride with Zach and his dad. Adam was a local like Zach, and lived within walking distance of the park, at his parents' place. He had a fantastic bedsit over their garage. Garth's student accommodation allowed him to rent year-round. He had a self-contained flat with its own bathroom and tiny kitchenette, which suited him down to the ground. His unit was one of several in a block, in an area of extensive student housing. Over the summer it was very quiet. Neither of his immediate neighbors had stayed for the vacation, so he could play his favorite Goth rock music as loud as he liked without upsetting anyone. He lived within a short stroll of the university library, which meant he could also get ahead with his coursework for the coming year. Physics fascinated him and he was looking forward to getting started on his dissertation.

He rolled his shoulders, groaning at the creaks. Cycling across town was not going to be fun. He did his final checks, shutting everything down. The last music went silent and colored neon turned to darkness. The quiet was a relief. Garth reached into his cubby to pull out his jacket and wallet then jumped at a touch to his shoulder. He yelped, banged his head on a shelf then fell back on his arse in an ungainly sprawl.

"What the..." He rubbed at his sore skull.

"Sorry, I didn't mean to startle you."

Garth raised his eyes to view his tormentor. His neck protested as he tipped his head back, then even farther back. He eyed the extended hand with suspicion but decided that, as he'd already made a complete idiot of himself, accepting assistance couldn't add to his humiliation.

"Can I help you?" Garth was pulled to his feet so fast he lost his balance and stumbled. The stranger steadied him with a hand on the small of his back. Warmth soaked through Garth's thin shirt.

"You okay? I don't want you bruising that cute backside any more than it already is."

Garth gulped before gathering his inner snark. "Do you think it's appropriate to be commenting on my arse? We just met. Who are you?"

Even in the dim light, Garth could detect the glint of amusement in steel blue eyes.

"Clem Chadwick, Sentinel Computer Services. Nice to meet you, Garth."

"How do you know my name?" Garth scowled, even though his traitorous dick was twitching with excitement.

"You mean, apart from the name badge pinned to your chest?" Clem chuckled. "Your boss told me. I have to install a patch on the ghost train computer and had to wait 'til closing to do it. He said you wouldn't mind hanging around for a few minutes."

"I suppose not — so long as it *is* just a few minutes. It's been a long day." Garth went to sit in one of the cars, feeling grumpy. "Help yourself. I haven't locked the cabin door yet, but you'll have to power up again." He didn't try to hide his irritation.

Clem quirked an eyebrow. "Quite the brat, aren't you?"

"Again with the personal comments! I'm tired and cranky. Sue me."

"Spank you, more like." Clem turned away with a grin.

Garth gaped. He was torn between running away and shouting *Yes, please!*

"Jesus. Fuck. I must be more tired than I thought," he muttered, watching Clem from beneath his lashes. The man was a vision in those black jeans and there was no harm in fantasizing. He drifted into a doze, imagining what it might be like to be under Clem's control, bound in his ropes, arse exposed for his hand or cane. In his dreams, there was no way that Clem would turn out to be either straight or vanilla. He shuddered and a small moan escaped his lips.

"I don't know what you're dreaming about, boy, but it looks good on you."

Clem was leaning over him. Garth blinked. He could smell mint on Clem's breath and the scent of his shampoo, he was that close. Garth scrambled from the car as fast as he could in an attempt to regain some dignity, but the erection crammed into his tight jeans didn't help. Nor did the knowing expression on Clem's handsome face.

"I've got the van," Clem said. "I'll give you a ride home." It sounded more like an order than a suggestion.

"My mother always taught me never to go with strangers. I've got my bike."

"Your bike will fit in the back of the van and I'm not a stranger. We've known each other for a whole hour. Ring Zach, or his dad. I'm an old friend of the family. They'll vouch for me."

Garth gave him a hard look. The thought of not having to pedal across town in the dark was tempting. He pulled out his phone and stabbed at the Speed Dial button that connected him to Zach.

"Hey, Zach. You know a computer guy called Clem?"

"Sure." From the sound of Zach's voice, he was trying not to laugh. "Gorgeous, isn't he? He was asking just the other day if you'd be back this summer. Not my type, but definitely yours. Dommy as hell. Has he got you in cuffs yet?"

"What the hell, Zach? He's just offering me a ride home and I want to make sure he isn't some psycho ax murderer." He caught sight of Clem, who had a huge grin on his face.

"Ride home… Yeah, sure. If that's what we're calling it nowadays." Zach made a sound somewhere between a snort and a grunt.

"Zach…"

"He's fine. I've known him for years. When I was a kid, he was a teenager and we knocked around together sometimes at family barbecues and stuff. He's a genuine Dom though, so watch that smart mouth of yours or he'll have a gag in it before you can say Goo Goo Dolls."

"Okay. If I don't show up for work tomorrow, the headlines in the local rag will be all your fault." He ended the call. "A lift would be good. Thanks." Clem's smirk was disconcerting to say the least. Garth covered his confusion by locking everything up. He rolled up his jacket then shoved it into his backpack with his wallet and phone. "Good to go."

Clem led the way to the staff exit at the southern edge of the park, using his security card to open the gate. His van was parked a hundred yards or so down the street. Garth liberated his bike from a long rack next to the curb before wheeling it to the rear doors of the van. Inside, the vehicle was immaculate. There was plenty of room to set the bike inside and Clem lifted it into position as if it weighed nothing.

Garth clambered into the pristine cab, wondering what the hell he was doing. There wasn't a wrapper or empty coffee cup to be seen — not a comfortable environment for someone as messy as him. Clem got behind the wheel and Garth knew there was no question as to whether the vehicle would start. It wouldn't dare break down. He fastened his seatbelt, very aware of the wide strap across his body, which seemed less like a safety device, and more of a restraint. He shivered.

"Are you cold? I can turn the heat up."

Garth shook his head.

"Use words, boy."

"Not a boy," Garth grumbled because he felt he had to, not because he really objected to the term.

"But you are a brat." Clem grinned.

"Screw you." The words were muttered, but Clem had the hearing of an eagle owl.

"Your mouth needs to be filled with something other than that language and believe me, if there's any screwing to be done, I'll be doing it."

"Don't make promises you won't keep." Garth made eye contact, knowing he was treading on very dangerous ground. The fine lines around Clem's eyes crinkled. His enigmatic smile didn't need the accompaniment of words.

"Where are we heading?"

Garth gave his address and Clem steered the van through quiet streets, avoiding the busier roads near the beach. He didn't attempt to make conversation, for which Garth was grateful. The silence wasn't uncomfortable and with Clem's solid presence beside him, Garth felt safe. When Clem pulled up outside Garth's block in the student village, Garth found he was reluctant to leave the warmth of the vehicle. The chill night air brought goosebumps to his skin. Clem opened the rear doors to lift out Garth's bike.

"Here you go. I'll see you tomorrow."

Garth positioned the bike between him and Clem, his backpack balancing on the saddle.

"You will?" A thrill of excitement set Garth's nerves tingling. Clem leaned across the bike, put a finger beneath Garth's chin and tilted his head with gentle pressure.

"I will."

Garth didn't expect the kiss that followed. It stole his breath and any ability to move. The press of Clem's lips was chaste but firm. Garth's cock stiffened and he whimpered. The temptation to beg for more rode him hard.

"Sweet dreams," Clem said, squeezing the nape of Garth's neck before he got back into the van.

As Clem drove away, Garth doubted his dreams would be sweet. They were going to be steamy, pulse-pounding, XX-rated... He wheeled his bike toward home, tripping a couple of times in his eagerness to get back. He didn't want to be excited about the possibility of meeting Clem again, but he couldn't help it. There was something about the man that called to him and one kiss would never be enough.

PUBLISHING

Sign up for our newsletter and find out about all our romance book releases, eBook sales and promotions, sneak peeks and FREE romance eBooks!

About the Author

Lucinda lives in a small village in the English countryside, surrounded by rolling hills, cows and sheep. She started writing to fill time between jobs and is now firmly and unashamedly addicted.

She loves the English weather, especially the rain, and adores a thunderstorm. She loves good food, warm company and a crackling fire. She's fascinated by the psychology of relationships, especially between men, and her stories contain some subtle (and some not so subtle) leanings towards BDSM.

LM Somerton loves to hear from readers. You can find her contact information, website details and author profile page at https://www.pride-publishing.com